PHA

FOLK

FOLK

ZOE GILBERT

BLOOMSBURY
LONDON · OXFORD · NEW YORK · NEW DELHI · SYDNEY

Bloomsbury Publishing
An imprint of Bloomsbury Publishing Plc

50 Bedford Square   1385 Broadway
London   New York
WC1B 3DP   NY 10018
UK   USA

BLOOMSBURY and the Diana logo are trademarks of Bloomsbury Publishing Plc

First published in Great Britain 2018

© Zoe Gilbert, 2018
Map and illustrations © Isobel Simonds, 2018

Zoe Gilbert has asserted her right under the Copyright, Designs and Patents Act, 1988, to be identified as author of this work.

Every reasonable effort has been made to trace copyright holders of material reproduced in this book, but if any have been inadvertently overlooked the publishers would be glad to hear from them. For legal purposes the acknowledgements on pp. 237–8 constitute an extension of this copyright page.

The following chapters were previously published, in slightly different forms, elsewhere: 'Earth is Not for Eating' in *Glint* (Glint Literary Journal, 2014); 'Tether' in *Thought X* (Comma Press, 2017); 'Thunder Cracks' in *Spindles* (Comma Press, 2016); 'Sticks are for Fire' in *Journey Planner and Other Stories and Poems* (Cinnamon Press, 2014); 'Fishskin, Hareskin', originally called 'Mawkin', in *Patria and Other Stories* (Cinnamon Press, 2015); 'The Neverness Ox-men' in *Gem Street* (Labello Press, 2012); 'Kite' in *Mechanics' Institute Review* (Issue 12, Autumn 2012); 'Water Bull Bride' in *What Lies Beneath* (Kingston University Press, 2015).

British Library Cataloguing-in-Publication Data
A catalogue record for this book is available from the British Library.

ISBN: HB: 978-1-4088-8439-3
         EPUB: 978-1-4088-8437-9

2 4 6 8 10 9 7 5 3 1

Typeset by Integra Software Services Pvt. Ltd.
Printed and bound in Great Britain by CPI Group (UK) Ltd, Croydon CRO 4YY

MIX
Paper from
responsible sources
FSC® C020471

To find out more about our authors and books visit www.bloomsbury.com. Here you will find extracts, author interviews, details of forthcoming events and the option to sign up for our newsletters.

For my mother

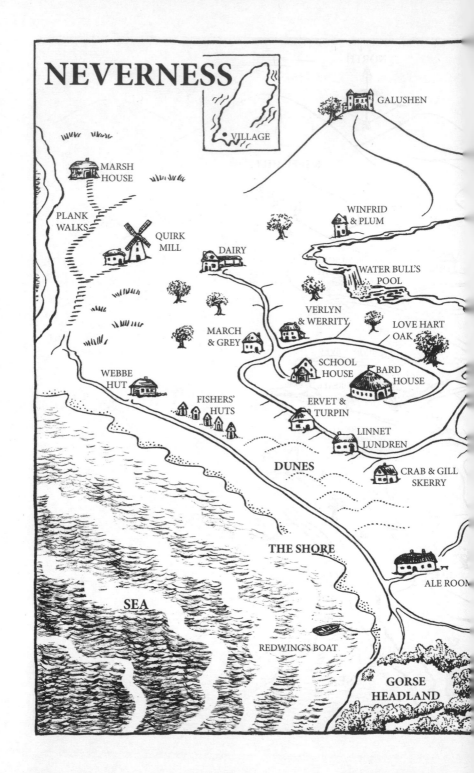

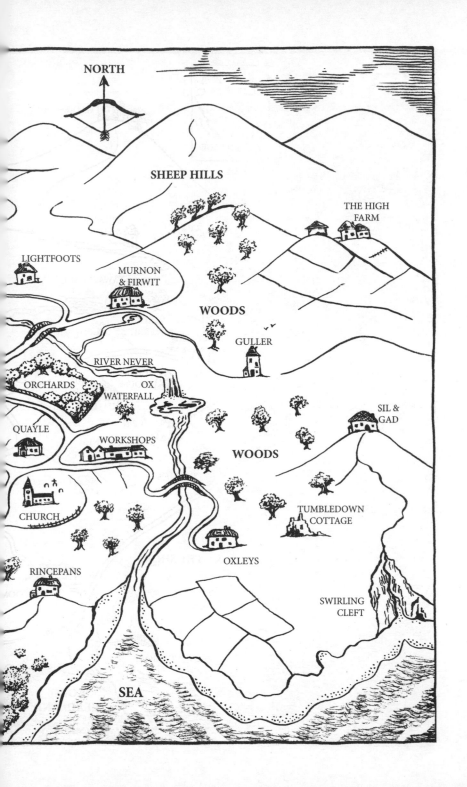

PRICK SONG

LISTEN, FOR THE BEAT that runs through the
gorse maze. It is an early twilight, the opening
between last sun and first star, the door of the day
closing until, soon, night will seal it shut. There are
feet thudding in the gorse's winding tunnels, hearts
thumping in time. Above them the breath of boys
hisses. Puffs of their steam are lost in spiny roofs. Their
arms are clad in sleeves of ox-hide, hairy and black.
The leather stinks. Elbows sweat. White shirts stick to
skin, and newly shaved heads bob, tender amongst the
prickly paths.

Four seasons of growth and the gorse has doubled
her spines. She has grown chambers and passageways,
whole rooms of thorn. She has twisted her maze so
cruelly that not one boy has been able to learn it.

Among the beating feet, Crab runs. His soles are
sliding on loose soil. He is a skinny stick of a thing,

taking his first turn at the gorse game. The bone shows through his pale scalp. He may be smallest, but he is fastest, skidding where the last of the golden flowers speckle sharp corners and hillocks. As the blue light deepens, he swivels at dead ends, ducks through scratching arches. Here and there, he passes other boys, thrusting leathered arms into the gorse, bare fingers fumbling, wincing as the thorns prick.

Crab has not dived yet. His eyes search the darkest parts of the gorse. When he finds what he wants, his dive will be headlong, the boldest of them all. *Gorse Mother*, he whispers, between hot breaths.

Look now, down the hill, below the prickly forest with its flickers of yellow petal, to where the girls are waiting. They stamp their boots in the heather. They twang the strings of their long bows, pretending at arrows, then stretch the strings until they snap. With these bows they have speared real arrows deep into the gorse, lodging amongst the thickest parts. The tattooed ribbons tied to them flutter against the gorse's black needles. Some girls have weighted their arrows with nails to make them go further and deeper. All of them have stitched their names on to the strips of cloth. A few have added a red dot, the thread broidered over and over to make a nub, which tells the boy who finds it that it is not only a mouth-kiss he will get when he returns.

All the girls want their kiss to be the reddest: a kiss from a boy who has dived so deep for her arrow that his lips have been pricked into a bloody pincushion.

Werrity Prowd gathers the other girls together. Her eyes are sly, her lips pursed into a pout. 'Who d'you want to kiss?' she asks each girl in turn: Plum, the orphan; Linnet, the golden harvest queen; March and Grey, the scowling huntsman's daughters. They laugh and whisper names.

The last to be asked is Madden Lightfoot, the stable girl. This year is her first with the arrow shooters. Her ribbon was the yolk yellow of gorse blossom. 'You can't choose who finds your arrow,' Madden says. 'And I won't tell who I'd want to kiss, anyway.'

Werrity sneers at her, crossing her arms over her round belly. 'Just because you're pretty, don't think you'll get the best boy. He's for me.'

'Hussy,' Grey hisses.

'Not had your fill of them?' asks March, and pokes Werrity's belly with the tip of her bow.

Turn away from the heather slope, to the seaward side of the hill. Sniff the air, catch the smoke. The men and women are already lighting torches, passing them along the line. All the villagers of Neverness are here: fishers and farmers, shepherds and huntsmen, fowlmonger, fiddler, brewer and beekeeper, seamstress, midwife, miller and bard. Every year they gather, while the girls shoot their arrows and the boys hunt them out, racing in the gorse. They are hungry for fire and begrudge the wait, but custom is custom. When the youngsters' game is over, and boys and girls are paired for the night, one kiss for each ribbon, they will make their thorny Gorse Mother blaze.

Come inside the gorse maze and take another taste of the lust that is driving feet faster on the paths. It is boys' lust for coy, buried ribbons. It is lust, too, for something darker. *Gorse Mother.* Night is falling and eyes are growing wild. There are whimpers as bare heads and leather-clad arms plunge into the nests of thorns. There are gasps at the thrill of pricking pain. Legs flail in panic when the spikes impale and trap a boy, who slithers out of his shirt. The others do not raise their heads as one runs from the maze, waving a beribboned arrow.

Down on the heather slope, Plum, the girl who made it, beckons him into the purple dark. The other girls crane to get a look at his lips, to know she will not cheat and bite her own mouth until it bleeds.

Crab is stumbling up there in the maze, ox-hide sleeves slipping down over his hands. He has seen the grazed head of the boy who ran down the hill. He has smudged the beads of blood that well from his own fingers. Retracing the warren, feeling for roots and twisted trunks he might recognise, he tries to find the ribbon that is lodged deepest.

He spots a white one, buried far inside a cave of thorns. It is more than his body's length away from the path. To reach it will mean more than scratches. Skin will tear. Crab balls up his hands inside the sleeves and pushes in.

Take a torch, the last to be lit, and follow the jostle of fat, spitting lights, as the men and women of Neverness spread out along the gorse edge. The air is riddled with spiteful shadows – the wounds and fears and furies of a village year – jinking between the people of Neverness, pulling their hair, tripping them up. The gorse-burning will smoke them out, cleanse the air for another season's turning.

Only a few girls still wait below, in the heather. Grey kicks at March's toes and they jab each other with their broken bows. Werrity Prowd still glowers, squinting for boys that might come flying down the slope. Madden stands apart, staring up at the sky.

'How many left, now?' a man's voice calls down towards the heather. The wind whips away his words and drowns them in the sea.

All autumn, Crab has twitched in his sleep, racing in dreams through the gorse maze, baffled by ribbons that slide away from his fingers. It is only on the day before the burning that he finds out what he must do to win.

Crab runs breakneck to the ale room, in time to find the trapdoor still wedged open. From the cellar come the shouts of boys. He slithers down into a tumult of flying shirts and ox-hide sleeves batted about heads. The cellar stinks of animal skin and boys' sweat, the fug of beer from the barrels. Crab ducks into the sack that is open on the floor and grabs the last roll of ox-hide. It is hairy and black, stiff as tree bark.

A boy Crab knows, Dally Oxley, sees him pick the sleeve up. 'They'll be a pair, if you can find the other,' he yells over the din. 'Take what you can get, I would.'

Crab nods and slides the hide on to his arm. It is loose, made for bigger bones than his. The broadest boys have taken the best sleeves and, with them laced on, duel with their forearms. He sees Sandy Rincepan sitting astride a barrel, while Drake, the handsomest of all the seven Webbe brothers, drags a blade through Sandy's hair, tufts of it feathering on to the floor. Most of the others have already shaved their heads. Dally Oxley points to his own bare skull. 'Do yours, if you want? Did Pie's for him just now.'

Pie is Dally's older brother by two years, but is twice his size. Crab shakes his head. 'Getting mine off tonight,' he says.

The fighting and yelling come to a halt. One of the boys has seen a face peering down in the light from the trapdoor and hushes the others.

'If Pie Oxley's down there, tell him I'm stitching a red dot thick as a currant for him,' the voice says.

Someone whistles from a corner. Drake Webbe calls, 'What about me, Werrity?'

'You'll be lucky,' the girl says, and vanishes.

'And those girlies think this is all for them,' Dally says to Crab. He balls up a crumpled white shirt and chucks it over. 'All so's we can beg a kiss off them and get half-flayed for it.'

'I'd not want a kiss off Werrity,' Crab says. All the boys have kissed Werrity Prowd. She helps her ma upstairs in the ale room, handing out sly looks with cups. Her mouth is always puckered into a pout, ready. But it is Madden Lightfoot that Crab has watched all autumn long. She is apprenticed beside him at the High Farm stables. Madden has grown taller and stronger than him the last few months. Her legs and arms are still bread-brown from a summer's sun. She is bolder with the horses. When she whispers into the colt's ear, Crab wishes it were him she coaxed.

'Nah,' says Dally. 'We'll give them girlies their kisses. But you want the same as what all of us want.'

Around Crab a chant begins to beat.

Gorse Mother, Gold Mother. Prick your mouth. Lick our spit.

The boys gather around Pie Oxley. He stands in the middle of the cellar, a head taller than any of them. Three times before he has run the gorse maze; his scalp and bare shoulders are covered in red freckles. He grabs the crotch of his trousers and mimes a groan of pleasure. Dally and the other boys whoop.

Gorse Mother. Gold Mother. Let me prick. Prick me back.

'She'll come back for me,' Pie shouts, and gives a deep groan, grinning all the while.

'That's what lucky is,' Dally yells to Crab over the thrum of chanting voices. 'Not a kiss from a girlie in the heather. You want the Gorse Mother to get you.'

Crab stares at the freckles on Pie's long, hard back as he turns around, raising his arms and beating his fists with the chant.

'Pricked him all over she did,' Dally says, close to Crab's ear, 'before he got his turn with the pricking. She's a mouth like a bowl of mulberries. All juicy. Swollen up fat from chewing on thorns. And she puts it on you and it's like ten mouths all at once. You go in the gorse and if she gets you, you come out a man.' Dally looks at his brother with envy. 'Bowl of mulberries,' he says.

The chanting goes on. *Gorse Mother. Prick Mother. Drink me deep. Drink me up.*

'How do you get the Gorse Mother?' Crab asks Dally.

'Got to be the bloodiest. Be pricked to pieces. She'll wait till the burning's nearly on her, and if you're bloody enough, she'll come.'

Pie Oxley has writhed his way to the row of beer barrels. He kicks the plug from one and catches the foaming spurt in a pail. It sloshes as he holds it aloft. 'Drink to the Gorse Mother. Drink to her and she'll drink you up!'

Crab idles along the wet sand, now that Ma Prowd has chased the boys from her cellar. He is walking towards his father's fishing hut. Along the way, he stops to plunge his head in the grey November sea, washing away the beer stink. He shakes the sea water out of his hair and shivers. He mouths Madden Lightfoot's name. But he whispers, *Gorse Mother.*

The first hut he passes is the Webbes', and sitting out on the step, huddled against the cold, is Verlyn Webbe. He eyes the ox-hide sleeves that Crab carries.

'Just saw your brother.' Crab nods towards the ale room. 'Aren't you doing the gorse game?'

Verlyn points with one hand to his other, misshapen, coat sleeve. Crab has seen Verlyn's wing plenty of times, in the schoolyard when they were smaller. 'Need two strong arms for that,' Verlyn says. 'Good luck.'

Crab bows his head as he sees his blunder. Heat floods his face. 'Sorry,' he mumbles, and hopes Verlyn did not hear his whispered prayer.

'Tell me what it's like, after,' Verlyn calls, as Crab walks on, into the wind.

When Crab pushes the door to his father's tarred hut, he finds him up to his knees in a tangle of nets. His father is Gill Skerry, a fisher stout as a barrel.

'Mending for next season,' he says when he sees Crab. 'Ready for a shearing, are you?'

They carry the stool outside and Crab kneels with the wind behind him, watching dark coils of his hair roll away along the sand from the blade of his father's knife.

'Tidy you with the razor when we're home. You'll be bald as an egg.'

Crab feels for the tufts on his scalp. It is not like Pie Oxley's red-freckled head, so high above his pincushion shoulders. 'You did the gorse-running, when you got to my age?' he asks.

'It's how come I kissed your mother.'

'But you didn't get freckles?' Crab's father's back is pale as a fresh piece of parchment. The only red that gets on it is from his wife's scrubbing, to scour off the smell of a night out fishing before he's allowed near the bed.

'Sure, I got a few scars from the stuff.'

Crab turns to look.

'All under here.' His father tugs at the matted broom of his own hair.

'And it made you a man?' Crab says. His face is burning red, sea salt dried around his eyes.

His father gives a sharp laugh. 'What you want is some hard graft and a few fights.' He grabs Crab's thin arms in his fists as if they were only the handles of a churn. 'I were stocky as a bull at thirteen. Didn't need a run through a patch of gorse to get my kisses. I seen you got your eye on that Madden Lightfoot. Well. At least you look less like a girlie with those curls gone.' He lifts Crab by the arms, runs out with him to the foamline and dunks him in the sea.

Come back now, up the rocks that loom above the shore, to where the men and women of Neverness wait with their torches. The sky above their heads is showing the first stars. The door of the day is nearly shut, but this is the hinge of the year itself. Days are shrinking, nights spreading.

Taste the fire and salt in the air. The game has gone on long enough. The gorse wants burning. Her scent may be sweet when her blooms bake in the sun. She may hold your washing out to dry with her pinching fingers. But she has a temper, and she will skin you if you do her wrong. The folk of Neverness want to hear her crackle, see her shrivel. They want to breathe her dying breath.

A white shirt streaks from the border of the gorse. 'How many left?' a man down the torch line shouts. It is Gill Skerry, Crab's father. 'Any girls still waiting?' One girl for each boy, one arrow for one bloody kiss. The wind up here roars in ears. It licks the torch flames into snarling dragons. Gill Skerry begins walking round the edge of the gorse, torch held low, heading for the heather to see for himself.

Another boy springs bleeding from the maze and pelts past Gill Skerry, down the hill. It is Pie Oxley. The ribbon he brandishes is yellow. When Pie reaches the heather slope, only two girls are left. Madden Lightfoot raises her hand to claim him, and Werrity Prowd gives a howl.

'How many left?' Gill Skerry yells higher up, his voice scattering in the dark. But Werrity is following Pie

Oxley as he leads Madden away down the hill, drawing her through a hole in the hedge to the next field.

Hear the anger in Werrity's voice. 'It's a mistake,' she cries. 'Pie Oxley is mine.'

Meanwhile, Gill Skerry raises his torch above the empty heather. Not a girl in sight. He tramps back up to the gorse edge. 'Let's get this done,' he shouts. The wind hurls his voice up to where a seagull screams, a white ghost in the dark. Torches lean in closer, their flames swooping at the gorse.

Crab is wriggling, a fish on a hundred hooks. His arms are stuck forward in their stiff hide sleeves. The ribbon he dived for is hidden now. It's too dark. There is blood in his eyes. He is caught by his trousers, by his too-big white shirt. The thorns are pressing through, piercing his skin. He has plunged deepest, stayed longest. He will be bloodiest.

Breath steams from him, hot and fast. His heart is thundering. He cannot hear his father's call to the torch-bearers. He cannot hear Madden Lightfoot say to Werrity, in the next field, 'Take him, then. It was Crab Skerry I wanted.'

Smoke rolls in and billows around Crab. He splutters. His body is sticky with sweat and blood. He hopes there is enough. He stops wriggling, and blinks to clear his eyes. Coughs are shaking his shoulders, heaving his chest.

In the smoky glow, Crab sees a shape in the gorse cave ahead of him. It brings its own light, a ragged black form against sunrise orange. She wears a crackling gown of thorns. Flowers bright as candles fly through it, from it. Her hair is thorn. Her eyes are amber. Crab lies still, pain giving way to warmth. Yellow fingers lick like flames. She takes him in her spiny arms and lifts him. It is like ten mouths on his belly. Heat pours down through his groin, his thighs. *Gorse Mother*, Crab whispers. *Eat me up.*

FISHSKIN, HARESKIN

Dew beater, Dew hopper,
Layer with the lambs,
Fiddle-foot, Light foot,
Skulker in the ferns.
Go-by-ditch, Go-by-ground,
Yellow speckled one,
Flincher, Snuffler,
Dweller in the corn.

'WHAT USE IS THAT?' Turpin says as Ervet struggles to lift the pot and swings it too quickly to the hearth, spilling water on to the stones. He is already gathering up cap and boots, stamping his feet on the gritty rug. 'What use, Ervet? Now I'll go without warming.'

Ervet watches him slap his arms and thighs, bending to peer through the window into the stubborn night.

'It's been a month now. Can't leave the bab with the wet nurse forever. Tell me you'll make peace and have your daughter home with you today?' The endless April rain scurries over the roof. Drips pat at the panes to be let in. 'Fox got your tongue, Ervet?'

A hare, she longs to say. *A hare got it*, but she bites the spite into her lip. It was one of the first lessons in Turpin's house: no speaking of hares, no thinking of them, even, if Ervet wished her new husband to return safe in his fishing boat. A hare is the worst bad luck for a fisherman. Whole nights, whole hauls, have been lost, because a fisher glimpsed a hare on his trudge down to the boat and turned right back.

Ervet knows every name for a hare that there is. She kept Turpin home that way, one night soon after they were wed. 'Dew beater, Fiddle-foot, Dweller in the corn,' she cried, and he had laughed as she pulled him back behind the box-bed curtain. It was that night, she was sure, in their bed that reeked of the sea, that Turpin planted inside her the gleaming herring that swelled in her belly, all winter and into spring, slithering and flicking its awful tail. How glad she has been to be rid of it, this last month.

The pot is still cold. Turpin is ready.

'Mother will come at sun-up,' he says, picking a seal-skin off the hook and shaking out the salt. 'And the wet nurse at midday.'

She bites harder on her lip.

'Be kind, Ervet. It's a kindness my mother does you. She said a spring clean will do you good.' He throws the sealskin about his shoulders. 'I thought we'd name the bab Iska, for her?' He leans to stroke her head and she flinches away from the fish-skin stink that is already on his hands. Turpin slams the door, leaving a spray of water behind him.

'Go-by-ditch, Go-by-ground, Skulker in the ferns,' Ervet mumbles, sinking back to sleep.

She is woken by her own name, bellowed. Ma Turpin has in one clenched fist a crumple of rags, in the other the handle of a pail. Soon Ervet is dressed in one of Ma Turpin's smocks, and all morning, while a bleary sun beckons beyond the cold stone walls of the cottage, Ma Turpin shows her what she does not wish to learn. How to scrub a hearthstone with sand to shift the herring grease. How to oil a sealskin just enough. How to sharpen gutting knives; how to gut and salt and thread so that always the smoking chimney will be hung with strings of curing bodies, like foul washing lines.

Ma Turpin's hands are barnacled with warts. When she scolds Ervet her voice is like a seal's bark. Turpin's clothes are crusted and unwashed, she barks. Turpin's cup is dirty. There is not enough soap, there is too much grime. 'What,' she asks Ervet, 'have you been finding to do all the long day that's more pressing than making spick and span for your husband?' They are standing in the garden, shaking out fish scales from the rug. Ervet looks over Ma Turpin's shoulder at the green hill. Beyond it lies the marsh and the sweet scent of rushes. It is there Ervet has crept, all those long days of biting winter and dank spring, with Turpin out on the sea and the herring curled inside her, heavier and heavier. On the marsh is her father's empty house, and she has left her fishwife tasks undone to go and mend its wind-blown slats, its salt-eaten floors.

'My son's one thing.' Ma Turpin is glaring at Ervet. 'But that bab's his own, which makes it mine, and I won't see it suffer in all this smirch. You see I won't.'

Ervet longs to drop the rug at Ma Turpin's feet and set out for the marsh, right now. But it is Ma Turpin who drops the rug and rushes past Ervet, for the girl Werrity has come with the shawl-wrapped bundle. Ma Turpin seizes it from her arms and brings it to Ervet, leaving Werrity on the path.

Inside the shawl, fishscale-patterned and smelling as much, are the grey eyes that never seem to close, just stare and stare at her, shining. There is the mouth that pops open and sucks at air.

'See that,' Ma Turpin barks, too close, her hot herring breath in Ervet's own mouth. 'It's your milk she wants. It's been a month now, Ervet. Time to take your turn, or your bab'll take that no-good teat girl for her own mam. And we all know she's nothing but trouble.'

Ervet glances at Werrity, who scowls from the path. Let her, Ervet thinks. Let her take the bab, fishskin and all.

'Ma Turpin,' Werrity calls. 'There's been a mishap up at the High Farm. The stable girl Madden's got bit by a horse and she can't staunch the wound. Looked a mess, and my brothers have ridden off somewhere.' She glares up at the hills above the village. 'Will you come and see?'

They both look at the bundle Ervet holds, then.

'You know what to do and what not to,' Ma Turpin says, less of the bark in her voice. 'You stay put with your bab and I'll be back round by tide turn.' She is asking Werrity has she salt, is the wound very deep, as they stamp away down the path. When their voices have faded, Ervet steps out after them and begins to walk, taking the other path through the dunes, towards the fishers' huts that line the shore.

. . · * ✳ · . . *

It was bafflement that made her father give Turpin his nod, in the end. Six herrings, Turpin had brought on the first day of courting, then twelve, and lastly twenty-four. They'd been laid out on the table, where her father had stared at them like rows of useless silver tools. *Worth that much to you, is she?* his narrowed eyes said. *More fool you.* Ervet had been glad to leave the smell of them and walk out with Turpin, to be his wife. A life with him could not be colder than one with her glowering father. The only sadness on that day, when the gift of fishes had done its trick and released her, was that her beloved hares could not follow her to Turpin's house. They had been her only comfort, at the silent marsh house. They had been a gift, too, one her father came to rue. He'd come home from hunting one day with bulging pockets. Ervet, still a girl, had screamed to see them squirm, believing he'd brought snakes, but when he'd let out the three tiny leverets, she had laughed as they bounded around her feet, hind legs already as strong as trap-springs.

＊ ☆ ＊

Ervet does not hurry through the ridge of dunes as she often has, darting between the tuffets of slicing grass. Instead she clambers up the sand, better to look at the shore. Out over the grey sea the cloud is low, ruffled like a deep belly of fur. The bundle is squirming against her shoulder, that same twist and lurch she felt when it was swimming inside her, when she was certain of its silver gleam and strong tail. The grey eyes match the sea so well. How can she name it? *Iska*, she tries, and spits the name out. She slithers down the dune on to the wet shore. Her feet leave dints that well with water as she walks.

＊ ☆ ＊

Her father loved nothing as much as his tools. He made the cunning trap that caught the leverets' blue-grey mother, and while Ervet coaxed the creatures from their corners that day, it was the scent of dark meat roasting that filled their draughty house. But he had let her keep them, and Ervet ate her hare supper with the three small bodies nestled soft as skeins of wool in her lap. Mawkins, she called them. She was only a child, then, and her favourite was the yellow-speckled one. He followed her about the house, while his grey sisters stretched themselves near the hearth, happy as dogs. She learned to smooth a finger along his scalp between his ears so that he would shiver and then lie still, letting her look into the puddle of his eye. When he beat his feet on hers she would lead him along the plank walk and up into the fields, where he ran his own mazes but always returned, to stretch his long yellow body beside her own, heart flickering under sun-smelling fur.

All three mawkins Ervet kept, and they grew with her. And on the blue bright morning after Turpin carried her away, she went back for them. She needed her dresses, her woollens and shoes, after all, but her yellow-coated friend and his sisters were more in her mind as she knocked and pushed the door. No father in his carved chair. No mawkins on the hearth rug. She followed the scrape and chuck of tools on wood through to the leanshed.

Two blue-grey pelts hung from the drying hook, blood black as tar dripping into a pail. On the workbench lay a yellow skin, piebald with purple stains, and beside it the skull, still flesh-streaked, still wet. Her father's eyes blinked at her where she blocked the light in the doorway.

'You've Turpin now,' he said. 'You'll not be needing these old pusses.' Ervet gripped the uprights either side of her, felt the wood grain slide through her fingers. 'Besides, they're the worst of bad luck to a fisherman.'

She stared into the dark of the skull's wide eye-hole until she and the leanshed and her father had all sunk inside it.

······· * ✿ ·· ·*

Ervet squats at the foamline, scooping bubbles into her palm, where they vanish. When water trickles on to the head in the bundle, the grey eyes blink but still stare at her, all clouds and sea. She lets the fishscale wrapping drop into the foam. The grey underlayer of swaddle is hot in her hands. Turpin is out on this same gritty sea, dragging up fish from their hidden swarms, dragging them up and bringing them home on his skin.

······· * ✿ ·· ·*

'It's no good, Ervet,' Turpin had said from behind the box-bed curtain, one night when, though frost still crusted the earth, she had slipped into the cottage from the deep dark of the small hours. She hadn't meant to stay so long at the marsh house, but the flushing of the reeds as she worked at her mending, hammering back the fallen slats, sealing the gaps with yellow marsh mud, had lulled her so, she had been able to forget the fish sleeping in her belly.

'We've a child coming,' he had said. 'Think of that. Where have you been?' She was silent. 'For pity's sake, Ervet.'

The curtain swept to one side and Turpin hauled himself up from the bed. He was still in the shirt he had put on in the chill of the night before, and as he moved towards her the stink of fish and sea seemed to wash right through her.

'Such a face! Is that your feeling, now, for your own husband?' He gripped her by the shoulders as she retched, her belly heaving, the fish inside churning, and when he tried to bring her close to him she pushed his chest.

Ervet had sat in the garden, then, breathing the night air clean and fresh as stream water, letting herself chill in it until the pinch of the cold faded. When the moon had sailed right across the sky and she no longer felt anything at all, not even a flicker of fishtail against her ribs, she stumbled indoors and set about lighting the fire. This much she could do. This she had done for her father, a thousand thankless times.

When she lifted the pot of water, pain tied a knot around her belly and pulled. She gasped, but did not drop the pot, and stood bent over until the knot loosened. When the pot was on and the fire steady, she was nearly at the box bed when the knot tightened again.

'Turpin?' she said. 'Turpin?' He woke with a grumble and looked right past her to the glow of the flames.

'That's better, Ervet,' he said, stretching, and got up to go and warm himself. 'We'll make a fishwife of you yet.' She let herself fall into the fishskin sheets and curled herself up there, listening to Turpin stamping his feet and splashing water across his face.

'Don't go out,' she called. 'Not tonight.' There was quiet and she knew he was bending to look through the window.

'It's calm as noon out there, Ervet. It'll be a good catch.'

'Please. Not tonight.' The knot was squeezing the breath from her. How to keep him here, how to make him untie it for her and bring her back to herself? 'Dew beater, Dew hopper, Layer with the lambs,' she cried out. 'Fiddle-foot, Light foot, Skulker in the ferns.'

The splashing and stamping stopped.

'You curse your own husband.' Turpin's voice was clenched. 'Then so be it. If you'd have the fish alive, swimming out beyond reach, and me dead.' She felt it then, the thrash of tail, and sea water poured from her. Turpin was gone.

. · * ✶ ·. *

The bundle squeals and writhes against Ervet. She remembers the knotted night, time tangling into day, then evening. It had been Ivy Rincepan who finally pushed open the door and found her. Ivy had set down her own pudding of a baby and used her hard hands, her hard grasp, to set Ervet free. 'You'll know what to do,' Ivy had said, lowering the squalling thing towards her chest. Ervet had shaken her head and turned away.

She takes another handful of foam, but when she looks up, along the shore, she lets the water seep through her fingers. There, on the black rock that runs down the shoreline like a charred spine, stands a hare. Its head is high, sniffing the sea wind that ruffles its yellow pelt.

'Dew hopper, Light foot, Layer with the lambs,' Ervet murmurs. The hare watches her as she steps along the thinning strip between the sea and seaweed line, past the Webbe brothers' fishing hut, towards the shore end. When she reaches the black rock, the sea has covered her path and lifted the seaweed up on its furling shoulders.

Ervet hefts her bundle higher. The hare takes the shore path in halting lollops, keeps on where the sand turns earthy and traces the edge of the marsh. When it reaches the point where the plankwalk juts out away from firm ground and into the reeds, the hare turns its puddle gaze on Ervet.

'Go home,' she whispers, but she walks alone with her grey bundle along the plankwalk, her feet finding the safe spots amid the broken slats.

Ervet unhooks the loop of plaited reed at the marsh-house door and breathes in the first deep draught of wind-dried wood and old smoke. The rosemary sprig lies on the table where she left it, browned leaves dropped and scattered across the wood she waxed. Beside it, the cradle basket the Webbe boy, Verlyn, had woven for her, still unused. She leaves the door open, for the wind, for the hare, and rosemary leaves scuttle across the floor. She flinches as she thinks of Ma Turpin's broom, of fishscales, of Ivy Rincepan's tut as she coddled two babs on her lap. But when she goes to lay her bundle in the basket, she finds she misses the heat of it against her breast.

She watches the bundle for a while. The marsh house is whole again, its wind-warped slats straightened, its rush roof wadded deep and dry. There is nothing left to mend. It is just as it was when her father vanished, a week after her wedding to Turpin. She'd supposed he was glad to be rid of her, and of her mawkins. Perhaps that was what he had waited for. She feels the chill the wind brings where her chest is still damp with sea water. The only part of the house she has not touched is the leanshed.

The door through to it hangs crooked on the salt-rusted hinge. On the threshold she smells rot, the green seep of the marsh water. The bench is bare; the hooks and ledges where her father's tools once glinted are all empty. But high in the corner, three pelts still hang, two blue-grey and one yellow. Cobweb knits about her fingers as she pulls one down.

She scrabbles in a drawer to find needle and thread, the finer kind meant for cloth and broken skin. Mother's work, stitching up. Her father had said this even as Ervet mended a slit in his palm, once, and neither had said she was no mother, not then.

The pelt is tough and soon speckled with her own red blood as she pushes the needle in, out, through. It is not dainty work. There are tears where her father was rough as he skinned. When she is done, she sucks the blood from her fingers.

'Flincher, Snuffler, Yellow speckled one,' she whispers, as she lifts her sleeping bundle from the basket and unwraps the damp grey linen. She folds around the pink skin a new, soft-furred one. The feel of fur warmed from within is soothing sweet. Ervet lies down on the old rug and folds herself around her mawkin.

THE NEVERNESS OX-MEN

I T'S WET IN THERE. Hark doesn't care. There's only a few drips get through the ox-hide, once you're in. It's the getting settled that's the slippery bit.

'If you get it wet, it stinks more,' his brother Dally once warned him, but Hark thinks a bit of beast stink will set things up nicely, make the girlies reel and pinch their noses.

He's listened to his older brothers quarrel on and on about the best kind of answers to what the girlies ask, which is nearly always the same. Just last week, he'd been swinging on the field gate with Dally and Pie, watching the black ox rip up daisies in the midday heat, while they debated just this question.

'The best way is to fright them,' Pie had said. 'That's what they want, it excites them. You seen what they get like at the gorse race.'

'Don't want to fright them like Crab Skerry did. Best stay alive,' said Dally, and both Hark's brothers had snorted with laughter.

'This in't like that, though,' said Hark, and tried not to think of that blackened boy in the gorse.

'Well, what you say depends on who it is comes along,' said Dally. 'If you get one of the pretty girlies, you want to make the most of it. Keep her there. When I got Linnet Lundren once, I kept her talking till that golden hair of hers was all frizzed up and her dress was wet through.'

Pie had pushed Dally off the gate then, into the dried rut of mud underneath, so Hark slid into his place.

'How do you scare them best?'

'She don't belong to you,' Dally grumbled, dusting off his knees.

'You have to think what it is girlies care about,' Pie said, and paused. Pie takes it very serious, but he's eight whole years older than Hark, so he's been doing it longest.

'Nice dresses?'

'That's one thing. But why do they like nice dresses?'

Hark thought hard. ''Cause they like things pretty and nice? 'Stead of interesting things?'

'Dally likes nice dresses, don't he?' Pie swung a foot at Dally and missed.

'When they're wet,' said Dally.

'They like pretty things,' Pie went on, 'because they think, if they look all frilly and act all lady-ish, they'll get married quicker to a handsome fellow and make a heap of babs just like their mammies. And that's what they want. Any dunnock knows that.'

'Babs?'

'Babs and a good soaking.' Dally had grabbed Hark's feet and somersaulted him backwards into a patch of nettles.

But here Hark is now, just him and the waterfall and the slime to get over. It's one thing avoiding the slews of green when you're in your trousers and you can watch your feet. When you're stitched into an ox-hide and you're too small to reach the eyeholes, things are more tricksy. It was bad enough bouncing against the tree trunks on the way through the wood, getting his feet in all the mushy leaves. Hark can't see any part of himself, and he nudges at the dripping rocks with his toes, trying to sense where there's grip, where there's slip.

It'll be like a room once he's in. There's so much water even this time of year that it makes a proper curtain, and the rush and splatter of it wipes out most other sounds. He can still hear a few dawn birdies in the wood waking each other up, telling each other how much they've got to do today, like his mam at the kitchen table. She'll be there now, spouting tea into Dally and Pie's mugs and making steam fly everywhere, hot steam, while the vapour in Hark's eyes is the cold kind. His stomach clenches for a moment, wishing for tea and a bit of honey bread, but you couldn't bring bread in here, it'd just turn into a soggy sponge.

The hide scrapes against the rock as he pushes himself the last few steps along the rock ledge, only treading on slime once and gasping as he tips, luckily inwards through the waterfall and not out into the swirling water of the pool.

He feels the water drench his foot and then stream over the hide and he skids on the other side and tumbles into the hollow head first.

Rolling sideways, he finds there is space and he can lie belly down on the upward slope of the cave with his face towards the sheet of white water. He manoeuvres an arm up and around and rubs his dented cheek. How long will he have to wait?

Hark wakes with a start when something raps on the hardened scalp of the ox-head. He blinks out through one eyehole. It's a slender, pink hand that withdraws through the fizzing curtain.

He hears giggling, and voices squabbling on the other side.

'Who will kiss Gertie Q?' someone calls.

He knows the voice. It's Plum, from further up the river. The one Dally went all soft over last summer. But Gertie Q? Hark tries to think.

'When we play the gorse game next, who will kiss her? Go on, then!' There is more giggling and Plum's hand comes through the water again and bangs the ox-head but he can't shift out of the way. He almost shouts 'Oi!' but remembers himself just in time. His head is all foggy, he can't think who that Gertie Q is, but they're laughing out loud and now he wants more than anything to be rid of them.

'Gertie Q won't never get a kiss, for she's a rattle-head.' Hark winces, he doesn't sound clever or scary, but then an idea comes and he adds, 'And anyway, no pretty dresses is going to fool nobody for she's that boot UGLY.'

There's no more giggling. Plum's voice calls, 'Gertieeee! Gertie!' There is scrabbling near his head and then Hark is left once more with just the hissing white waterfall.

Nobody else comes. While Hark lies in the ox-hide, which really is stinking worse and worse the damper it gets, he tries to think who Gertie is. There's nobody in Neverness he doesn't know, or at least know about, and as he wanders around the village in his head he sees her all in a rush. Gertrude from the Quirk mill on the marshes, who's shorter than her younger sister. Gertrude whose hair is all in short black tufts where her ma hacks it off so the wind won't blow it into knots. Gertrude whose little thin back is skewed bent far worse even than Verlyn Webbe's, and she has to put a box on the school bench to get her nose above the books.

Hark feels all of a sudden how cold he's got in all that waterfall vapour.

It's a bigger battle getting back out than it was falling in, but at least the struggle warms him a little, and he doesn't care about the dark that knits the wood together now because he's on his way home. He knows the path blind, but the sight of the small window full of yellow light makes Hark feel a bit whimpery again.

He hurls himself and the ox-hide on to a pile of hay in the barn and crawls out backwards. He reeks all over and the sharp stench follows him into the house where they are all waiting, Dally and Pie and Ma and Pa. He is proud as punch when Ma pours the tot of whisky all grandly in his steaming tea and they each slap him on the back, even if Pie does wipe his hand on his trousers after.

Ma leads the toast, 'To Hark, our newest Ox-man!' and her cheeks are still red when she doles out the special stew she's made, with sausages added like he asked for. Hark chews through the juicy, fatty meat, feeling like he is nearly at being a man, now that he can do the waterfall like the rest of them, and maybe he'll even beat Dally at an arm wrestle soon if he keeps practising. He tries not to think about Gertrude and her bent little back.

After the sausage and the whisky and being warmed thoroughly through, Hark is so sleepy that he can't even stand for a scrub-down and Ma lets him fall into bed as he is. He drifts away thinking of the cleverest things he will say next time he's in that ox-hide, all about babs and marrying and girlies and dresses.

When Hark wakes in the dark, he thinks it must have been Pie's grizzling snores, or Dally's whistling ones, that did it. He huddles down deeper under the blankets, catching a whiff of hide that makes him grimace, when a thump comes from below. There are voices bobbing about down there. Opening one eye, he sees the moon peering back at him through the pane.

The stair creaks and Pa's whisper darts into the room. 'Pie, get up and find yer boots.'

Pie grumbles out of sleep and away down the stair.

Standing at the window, Hark sees two lanterns swooping away from the house like will-o'-the-wisps. Why have they gone off without him? He's a man now, nearly; an Ox-man anyway. Dally might be as useless as wet pastry, but not him.

Ma is at the hearth, digging her heels into the embers and rubbing at her arms, though it's not so cold for night-time.

'What's they all up to?' he asks her, trying to sound serious like Pa.

Ma sighs. 'A bitty girl's gone missing and there's a search out. Sent your pa and Pie along to help, though it's likely nothing but high-jinks.'

'Who's that then?'

'Quirk's child from the mill. She's at the school house with you, Pie said. Not Bryony, the other one.'

'Gertrude?'

'That's her.'

The puff goes out of him a bit and he feels a heavy weariness in his bones like he could fall in his bed and sleep for a night and a day, but he throws the blanket from off his shoulders and declares he'll join the hunt.

'You'll do no such thing,' Ma growls. She is just like a bear sometimes and she knows it.

'I must,' says Hark. He can't tell her about the little cold egg of ache that lodged in his stomach after the waterfall and has been growing, until now, at Ma's news, it feels like it has hatched into an ice-dragon that is sweeping its icicle tail around inside him. He was just trying to scare the girlies, like Pie said. And they were goading him, putting their hands through, rapping on his ox-head and giggling, and he had to think too fast and he hadn't thought who Gertie was before he yelled at them. All this stays stuck in his throat.

He climbs the stair without saying a word, pulls his boots and his cap from under the bed as silently as he can while Dally whistles away in his sleep. Then he climbs up on the bedstead, pushes the hatch to the loft and hauls himself up.

At the back of the house there's as much holes as there is roof, and Hark can see the stars beckoning him out into the night. He ducks through an easy hole at the bottom, and with a quick dangle from the cornerstone he drops into the dew-wet grass.

He blunders into a bucket halfway round the house and it clangs like a church bell. One thing the others have got that he hasn't, he thinks, is lanterns. But it's too late now. He's out, he's helping the search for poor Gertrude Quirk and that's all, so he follows his feet, which take him along the path he knows blind, through the woods towards the waterfall.

The invisible trees along the path are so quiet that he can hear the water whispering from far off. It confuses the wood, makes the waterfall closer and then far away, and the familiar root shapes and winds in the path mix about so he stumbles once, and then again. How do you search for a bitty thing in the pitch dark? He should shout her name, but he feels daffy when he hears his voice so small and muted, swallowed up straight away by the wood.

When he enters the clearing, he sees the pool made silvery by the moon and feels his cheeks getting damp with mist. Hark sits on the soft moss that soon soaks a wet patch into his trousers, and tries to think.

There are so many water sounds in the dark: drips from the creeper, the stream like girlies' giggles, the white water rushing over the cave. He stares at the silvery black eddies in the pool, the ribbons of moon water that keep sliding about under his eyes.

Where would Gertrude, with her little bent back and her blackbird-chicky hair, go in the middle of the night? Maybe, if you're a girlie and you might be crying – for that is how he pictures her now – you want to go where there's other wet things dripping water, so as not to feel so alone.

Maybe, if it's worse than a girlie crying and she is so sad and ashamed and never wants to see anyone ever again in case they call her boot ugly, she'd come here too. Hark stares into the water. He knows how deep the pool is. You wouldn't even have to be small to get lost down there. The water sounds of smashing and slapping seem to get louder and louder until he can't stand it any more, he can't think any wise thoughts, only black, night-time, deep-water ones, so he jumps up and begins edging around the slime ledge towards the waterfall.

Hark skids, grabs some overhanging creeper and practically swings through the wall of water, landing in a slithery tangle on the smooth rock behind. In the untangling he realises not all the arms and legs in the knot are his own. Hark yelps. Something yelps back, but it's not his echo. He pedals his legs and wind-mills his arms, trying to push himself back up the slippery rock, grazing his elbows, frantic with trying not to feel whatever the soft, lumpy thing is that he has touched.

'Ow!' it says. It's more whimpery even than Hark. 'Stop kicking me!'

He catches his breath. 'Who's that?' he says.

'Who's that?' the thing sniffles.

'Hark.'

'Hark what?'

'Hark Oxley.'

'Oh,' it sniffs. It sounds like a huffy girlie.

'I'm hunting for Gertrude Quirk,' he says, importantly.

'Well, bully for you then. Here I am.'

Hark blinks in the dark but he can't see a thing. He tries to rub his sore elbows and slides back down the rock where his knees hit some other, smaller knees.

'Ow! Stop that!'

'What are you doing here?' he asks, scrambling backwards.

'I came to see what's behind this dog-stupid water-fall,' she says, 'and give it a piece of my mind.' She sounds a bit like Hark's ma when she is being a bear.

'Are you sure you're Gertrude Quirk?'

'What sort of dog-stupid question is that? Just what I'd expect from things that lurk in caves.'

Hark is vexed. This is not what he expected to find. This is not at all what he thought Gertrude Quirk would turn out to be either, who never makes a squeak on the school bench, and what's more, she has just called him stupid, twice. The vexing feeling pinches at him until he yells at her, 'I'm not stupid! Not now and not today neither. I had to say something to scare girlies and so that's what you got.'

He pulls a face at her in the blackness and feels better, for a moment, until she replies, 'You? It was you, Hark Oxley?' She laughs a loud, cackly laugh while Hark's heart sinks like a cold stone into his belly.

'Well, no wonder, then,' Gertrude manages between cackles. 'No wonder it weren't scary at all!'

Hark blurts, 'You mustn't tell. Never, never ever until the moon turns blue, or it drops out of the sky, you mustn't.'

Gertrude stops laughing. 'Why not?'

'You know straight why. Nobody but an Oxley's supposed to know who's in there.'

'I don't see why I should keep it hidden,' she says. 'How'll I ever keep a serious face in the school house?'

'You've got to. Please, Gertrude. I'll do anything you want. I'll give you rides on the dray, and I'll let you up into Dally's tree-hut and you can have my ma's honey bread she gives me for my school tea any time you want.' He regrets that last one, but it's too late. This is bad enough that he'd be giving up a lifetime of honey bread if his ma and pa found out.

'All right,' Gertrude is saying, 'I won't tell if you let me try.'

'Try what?' He hopes she means riding the dray horse.

'Let me wear that ox-hide and let me sit in here telling people horrors about their fates like you do.'

'You can't. No girlies can and specially ones that aren't Oxleys neither.'

'Of course I can. And if I can't, I'll tell.'

They sit in the endless rush and splash of the waterfall, in the bottomless black of the cave, and Hark knows he is defeated by little Gertrude Quirk.

It's a week before Hark gets another turn at the water-fall. He finds Gertrude waiting by the pool, and he warns her about the stink but she doesn't whinge like he supposed a girlie would, not about that or the hard scratchy skin. She doesn't even slip on the slimy rock.

There's not much room for the two of them stuffed inside the ox-hide and Hark is nervy at feeling Gertie so close. They lie in the cave, listening to the drips and splashes.

'If it's girlies that come,' he says, 'you've got to scare them about getting married and babs.'

'Bog water,' Gertrude replies. 'What's scary about that? There's much better things to put them in a spin. I know. I've been practising on Bryony for all my life.' Her little dark eyes are looking wily.

'Well, that's what they'll ask. It always is,' says Hark.

They are arguing about what noises a fortune-telling ox should make, growls or snorts or gnashing sounds, when they hear voices on the other side of the whitewater curtain.

'I'll ask for you and you ask for me,' a girlie's voice is saying, all singsongy.

'Well, don't ask silly then, or it's wasted. And I'm asking first.'

'No, I'm to ask first, I'm eldest.' They sound uppity as a pair of magpies.

'That's Plum,' Hark whispers.

'And Madden Lightfoot,' Gertie hisses in his ear. 'Her sister Clotha says she's soft in the head.'

'What should we do—' Hark begins, but Gertrude interrupts with a roar that makes his ears rattle. The girlies outside squeal. 'You're supposed to just whisper what to say,' says Hark, feeling vexed again. 'I'll do the ox voice.'

'You said you'd let me,' mutters Gertrude.

'Ox! Oh, ox!' Madden's voice calls. Gertrude smirks. 'Tell us, oh ox, who will kiss Linnet Lundren in the gorse game? And fall in love and marry her forever? Will it be... Drake Webbe?'

Both Hark's brothers are moony over Linnet Lundren and her long yellow hair. And he knows Drake too, the handsomest of all the Webbe brothers who dive in the sea like black-headed seals. If anyone was going to marry Linnet Lundren, it would be Drake Webbe.

Gertrude roars again and before Hark can stop her she is bellowing with all her might.

'Linnet Lundren's hair will all fall out. Her teeth will turn black and the smell of her breath will turn to rotten eggs.' There is a shriek from outside. 'And Drake Webbe won't marry nobody for he'll go so mad from diving deep that he'll think he's a real seal and he'll get chewed up by a whale.'

Hark stifles his laughter as Plum and Madden howl on the other side of the waterfall.

All day Gertrude and Hark make up nasty fates for their visitors, and they become more wild and grisly the more practice Gertrude gets.

The hide is soon heated with their laughing, and Gertie makes Hark jump when she pokes him in the ribs, so he pokes her back, though not as hard as he pokes at Dally and Pie. They are still there when the dark lays its felt through the wood and the moon's eye lights on the clearing, turning the waterfall into a wash of silver. It gleams as it gushes beyond the warm ox-hide, sending its ripples shivering across the deep, black-water pool.

'If you swear you'll never tell, you can be a secret Ox-man, long as you want,' says Hark.

'I'll be the first Ox-woman,' Gertie replies.

'All right. But swear you'll not tell my ma. Nor your sister, neither.'

'Never.' Gertie roars once more, and they listen to its echo in the dripping cave, until it's time to begin the tricksy journey out over the rocks and into the wood.

THE TRUE TALE OF JACK FROST

'ONCE UPON A TIME, there were two sisters,' said the teller. 'Neither was a very good girl, but their mother loved the younger sister best. Even in winter, when the sky filled with feathers and the water turned to glass, it was the older sister who had to do the chores.

'"You've sharp elbows," their mother said. "Go and crack the ice and bring me water." When the girl came back with a full pail, their mother said, "You've toenails like claws. Go and kick up the turnips from the garden."'

Squashed under the beams at the back of the bard house, the girls of Neverness sat in a row, so they might whisper and nudge and pass their secrets. Amongst them was Grey, jiggling her knees in the gloom beside March. They sat far from the fire and the teller, but still her older sister's cheeks glowed. Grey looked about at the rapt faces of Linnet, Plum, Madden and Werrity. None glanced back. Then she pinched March's thigh and leaned close to her ear. 'When the girl came back with the turnips,' she sang, matching the teller word for word, 'her fingers all black, their mother said, "You've a fire in your head. Set the hearth and make us warm."'

'Shhh,' March hissed, pinching her sister back. 'It's not your tale.'

'Every winter, the same ones.' Grey rolled her eyes. Madden elbowed her from the other side.

'Who's that?' came the teller's voice from the far side of the fire. 'Who has broken the tale, when I've begun?'

Grey waited as heads turned, the crowd looking back into the shadow where she and March had settled near the door. The other girls looked down at their laps.

'It was her.' Grey pointed. With her other hand, she yanked March's red plait down her back, so her face tipped up for all to see.

'One more trick, you'll be out,' said the teller, squinting into the dark. 'Now, I'll begin again. This is the Tale of Jack Frost.'

'Just listen,' March whispered and shifted further into the corner. Grey leaned back against a beam and let the icy draught from the doorway chill her cheeks. The other listeners gazed once more into the fire, while the familiar words droned on. Grey put her fingers in her ears and made a story of her own.

When March flew into the house and clanged the water pail down on the table, Grey stared at her sister's cheeks and chin, red raw. She went for a closer look.

'If you'd been out in the cold,' said Grey, circling her sister. 'But this January's suddenly mild as May.'

March dipped her finger in the pail and flicked water at Grey.

'So, who's been kissing you?' Grey poked her sister's red sore chin.

'Oh, Jack Frost!' March said, and fled up the stairs.

'I sent you for water at noon,' their mother yelled from the garden, where she had dragged the rocking chair and rug. Grey looked out and saw their mother, curled in Father's lap in the chair. Where there had been snow only a few days ago, sparkling hard on the ground, the rockers now sank in wet mud. Instead of frost, there were weeds speckling green in the turnip patch.

The next day, Grey spied on her sister as she took the wrong turn from the house with the empty pail, and she followed her. How March swung her arms and threw back her head as she sped right away from the gurgling river and up towards the wood. She didn't hear one squelch of Grey's feet in the melt puddles. She didn't turn when Grey cursed the drips from the thawing trees. Deeper into the wood they went, where ramsons waved their green ribbons by the path. March slowed, ambling in the eager January sun.

Grey trod on a snowdrop as she went to skulk behind a sturdy oak tree. It was not long before she heard her sister shriek, and peeped round when the shriek turned to a laugh. She saw, wrapped around her sister's waist, the long, pale fingers. She saw the man's shirtsleeved arms lift March high and swing her, as she gazed down at his thin, white face. The lovers' eyes gleamed. The air around them sparkled. Grey felt a cold prickle at the crown of her head. As she watched, it spread all the way down her neck, her back, through her buttocks and belly, her thighs, her knees, her toes. She pressed into the oak tree trunk and stared at the man until he was frozen into her mind's eye, slender and graceful and hard and so very pale. Grey crept home, relishing the drips from the trees that trickled over her scalp.

'It was noon when I sent you for water,' their mother bellowed from the garden.

'It's me,' said Grey. She found their mother lying alone in the rocking chair, and she sat in her lap and wrapped her arms around her neck.

'Your father's gone hunting,' her mother said. 'Every January since we were wed I've had him all to myself, bless the snow. But this thaw has made his old fingers itch.'

'I want a lover, too,' said Grey into her mother's shoulder. 'I'm too old for silly kissing games in the gorse.'

'Has that Oxley boy not come courting?'

'Pie? Too spotty.'

'Or the Rincepans' lad?'

'Sandy? Too round.' Grey shuddered.

'Your turn will come, my bonny girl,' said her mother.

'I want the lover that March has got.'

Her mother pushed her upright, better to look into her face.

'She doesn't go to the river, or to the well, Mother. She goes to the wood and waits. I've seen him. He's splendid.'

'The tyke,' said her mother. 'So, what is he like?'

Grey told.

Her mother tapped her fingers on the arms of the rocking chair. 'Your curls may be mousy and those freckles can't be helped, but you're still bonnier than March, my girl. If you want him, I'm sure all you have to do is wait in her place.'

'But March will be swanning off there the moment you set her a chore, Mother.'

'She won't. I'll put her to sweeping the cellar first thing, and I'll shut the trap. I'll say I forgot she was there.'

'What if she knocks?'

'I'll say I didn't hear.'

Grey kissed her mother's cheek, and together they basked in the sweet winter sun.

When March came home, nobody said a word as she clanged the pail down on the table. Grey still said nothing when March steamed up the whole house, boiling all the water for a bath, which she sat in right through the evening until it was cold. Grey drew long fingers in the misted windows and imagined them curling around her waist, lifting her up in the air, twirling her like a top.

She spied on March as she dressed and saw her put on new stockings, new boots of black fur, new gloves fresh as snow. 'Where d'you get those?' she said, blocking her sister's path down the stairs.

'Out of my way,' said March, and twisted Grey's ear.

'It's night, dear sister. You must stay home, safe. But really, where did you get those?' Grey nudged at March's furred feet with her toes.

'Oh, from Jack Frost!' March cried. 'Let me go,' and she pushed past her sister, tripped over Grey's out-turned foot and tumbled down the stairs.

Their mother came running. 'Help me put her to bed,' she said to Grey, while they both made eyes at the new boots and gloves. They gripped March's arms as they helped her back up the stairs. She made a terrible noise, spluttering and howling. When they had tucked her as tight as they could under the covers, they locked the door and listened to her snivelling.

'The tyke,' said their mother. 'She'd better stay put tomorrow. No chores for her. Take these.' She gave Grey the white gloves and the black fur boots that she had pulled from March's hands and feet. 'Now come and keep me company. Your father will be out hunting all night, and since it's January, I will miss his old bones.'

So they got into the big feather bed, and chattered, and whispered, and snored into the night. Under their deep, downy quilt, neither of them noticed how the air chilled, and the world outside grew quiet.

When they woke in the morning to the hammering of March's fists on her door, they saw that Grey's scribbles had gone from the windows, replaced by patterns of glittering trees and frosted leaves. They hurried down the stairs, shivering, away from the din. Grey opened the door and saw snow as high as her knees, crumbs of it sailing in eddies through the blue air. She watched her breath mist and her fingers turn pink.

'Doesn't look like stopping,' said her mother behind her. 'And your father still out in those woods.'

'March won't stay put much longer,' said Grey.

'I'll do my best,' said her mother, as she held out the boots for Grey's feet and the gloves for Grey's hands. 'And he does sound splendid, even apart from the gifts.' She waved her daughter off. Then she sat by the cold grate, biting her nails and saying to herself, 'He should be back, he should be back by now,' while March raged and stamped above her head.

Grey kicked her way through the snow so it fell again like clumps of feathers. The trees, decked in icicles, were not so familiar as yesterday, but she found her way. Her boots crumped in the thick quiet and were soon damp. The gloves, too, were soon wet with brushing snow from her hair. But her cheeks were surely glowing. She would look very bonny indeed as she waited on the path near the broad oak.

Grey waited and waited, snowflakes sailing about her. Her toes turned numb. She tired of batting the blizzard from her face and let the flakes settle, hardening on her lashes. Her eyes were surely sparkling. She bit her lips to keep them pink. Then she tried a little laugh, but it turned into a gulp. Still nobody came. She tried to wriggle her toes, but they were frozen solid. Her fingers would not move in the stiffened gloves.

She began to walk, further into the wood, to warm herself, and so that she might find him sooner, while she could still make a winsome smile. She followed the path as the trees crept in closer, webbed together by drifts of snow. The path petered out. It meant pushing between holly bushes, shoving through the drifts that hid bramble traps to trip her up. But it didn't matter, because even though her teeth chattered and crystals weighed down her eyelids, she found a kind of cabin. It was more of a hut, really, in size, but it was hard to tell because it was all over icicles, hanging from the roof to the ground, thick as glass trunks. Its roof glittered with frosted snow.

Grey shuffled around the ice cabin until she found a door, with a slit of window in it. She pressed her icy nose against it and spied inside. There, sitting quite upright on a wide, silvery bench, was the man. He had long, pale fingers that twiddled in his lap. His thin, white face was turned towards the door.

He gave Grey his arm as she hobbled inside. Her mouth made a smile, lips closed to hide her chattering teeth. There was a sound of crackling, just like a warm fire, but Grey did not see any hearth inside the cabin. There were no rugs, no furs, only the bench and a small table on the other side. On the table stood a lantern that burned with a chill blue light. Grey swayed on her numb feet, but the man caught her, his long fingers at her waist.

'My bonny girl,' he said. Or Grey thought he said this. His voice was so hoarse as to be a whisper that misted in her ear. 'Let me help you.'

He tugged the white gloves from her hands and tossed them on to the table. He unhooked her coat and peeled it from her shoulders. Then he strode to the bench and sat, straight, looking at her with eyes so pale they were hardly blue. Grey was colder than ever, in the crackling cabin with no fire.

'Your boots,' he whispered. And Grey had to shamble, as prettily as she could on her numb feet, towards the bench. He patted the seat and eased her on to it. His smile was wide across his narrow face. She waited as he bent and tugged each boot from her foot, left, right.

'Who gave you those?' he asked. His breath made no mist. 'Who?' The man slid closer to her on the bench.

His thin arm pressed against hers and made her tremble all the more.

'Um, Jack Frost?' Grey said.

His fingers were hard at her waist, turning her towards him; his face, so close, the bluish white of early morning snow. He was splendid.

'Jack Frost,' Grey said again, leaning back a little, against his hands. Her eyes were wide open as he pressed his mouth to hers, parting her lips. Her eyes stayed open as he breathed into her, a breath of ice that frosted her lungs and froze her veins.

There Grey sat, when he had pulled away. Her mouth was wide, her eyes startled. She was leaning back a little, against the air.

After she had tugged at the door handle until it tore off and kicked at the door until her toes broke, March lay on the floor and howled herself hoarse. That took a little time. Then she lay quiet, listening to the throb of her bruises. The door hung heavy on its thick black hinges. She crawled towards it and started with the lowest hinge, twisting the screw with her fingernail.

As she turned the ninth and highest screw, a nail torn for each before it and her fingers stained with blacking, she heard voices outside the house. From her window she saw the snow falling, and the beautiful endless blanket of it, torn by the footprints of three men. They were carrying her father into the house. March wrenched the door from its hinge and stumbled down the stairs.

Her father was laid out on the table. Her mother and the men bent over him.

'What's this?' asked March, but her mother only moaned.

'Found him by the wood,' one of the men said. 'Blizzard came in so fast last night. Must be he thought to sit it out.'

The ice in her father's beard and eyebrows was starting to melt. Water dripped on to the table. Her mother bent lower, until her lips touched the water.

March stared at him, until the cold from his body crept over her own skin.

'Where's my sister?' she said. 'Where's Grey?'

'Once upon a time there were two sisters. They were as bad as each other, but neither was as bad as their mother.'

March looks out across the bard house fire, at the rows of faces turned towards her. So many nights she has fidgeted her way through tales, yawned at the tellers, yet here she is. Her palms are sticky. She glances towards the shadowy patch by the door and breathes deep.

'When winter came,' she goes on, but she hears a whispering from the back of the bard house. 'Who's that?' she recites. 'You've broken the tale, when I've just begun.' She squints into the dark. A narrow, pale face leans forward from the shadow. It is lit by a lantern burning blue. March's tongue turns dry.

'I'll begin again,' she says, keeping her eyes on the bard house fire, its orange flames, the rosy faces nearest. 'This is the tale, the true tale, of Jack Frost.'

STICKS ARE
FOR FIRE

A CURED STICK FOR *a stirrer. A sturdy one for*
a sweeper. Brittle sticks for tinder. A green branch to
hang the pot. A forked one for ceremony.

I chose my sticks with wisdom. It were a green day, a bird
sang, I remember, while I walked up. Unwound the ivy,
careful, and noted the turn of the coil. Sunwise a good sign
for a merry-weather stick, widdershins for doing the darks.
Two forked sticks, among all those sticks that were mine.
And then those small pink hands holding them, like mole
paws before the skins are dried out. A mole paw is good for
an earth curse, or to find the way in a moonless night. What
moon is it tonight? My bones can't tell me. Cover my peepers
and I can see most things, just ask me, but now I see noth-
ing. Those were my sticks, in those small pink hands. They
were my bones, my skull, my fingers, and those of them that'll
waggle still I've walked about me and I've felt a bit of what
the sticks have done. There's pulpy parts, sticky messes. What

was wet has dried to crusts, mostly. Some fingers are stuck together with it. Eyes gummed tight shut. That's if there's still eyes, under these crackly lids.

'Who told you such a tale?' Shilla Quirk rears up from the earth wild-eyed and brandishes her spade high in the air, sending a hail of soil over her two daughters. 'Who told you and how much?'

Bryony glares at Gertrude, but she has on that mask she can conjure sometimes that makes her into a dolly, silent and with painted-on eyes. Around their mother's feet lie stones and dandelion roots like witches' fingers, torn from the vegetable patch. Bryony thinks of mandrakes, their silent screams, and the screams that echoed in the story they have heard. She wants more; for the shadowy horrors to be brought out into the chilly light.

'It were Guller the fowlmonger,' she mumbles. 'We went for the eggs like you asked and he gave us some pretty feathers, too, and...'

'It were Guller.' Shilla shoves the spade down into the clumpy earth at her feet where it splits a root with a crunch. She rubs her huge hands over her face, and when her arms drop down her features are changed. Her bulgy eyes look tired. 'That's folk for you,' she says, eyeing the broken ground.

Neither Bryony nor Gertrude make a sound. There's nothing at all but the daft cheeps from the nest in the wych elm and the hush-hush of its bright new leaves. Bryony bites on her thumb and thinks how her lips would feel if they were in that tale they'd heard, split and squishy as gone-over raspberries.

'Is it true, then?' asks Gertrude. Bryony wonders where she gets that stone inside her from, even though she's so small; how she can squash the fear like a frog under that stone that gets them both into such trouble.

Shilla squats down and takes a handful of soil, rubbing it between her fingers to test its goodness. 'It were a long time ago, so long now it don't matter so much, but it's a lesson for you meddlers, in its way.'

'What's the lesson?' says Gertrude. Her black hair is sticking out in tufts from her bony head, and Bryony thinks of moss on a small boulder.

Shilla heaves herself upright and gazes at the girls. 'Spades and forks, the pair of you. Get your pinnies on and follow the furrow behind me.'

'Do you think she'll tell?' Bryony whispers to Gertrude as they carry the tools back to the garden.

'I'll make her tell,' says Gertrude. 'Don't you want to know?'

'I don't want a bruise for the school house tomorrow.'

'Don't be such a rabbit-bottom. It'll be worth it. And it were real people who lived here who did it, and a real witch. Hark showed me her old house near the woods, all crumbled.'

'Just keep that tongue of yours in your mouth if she gets uppity.'

Gertrude glares over her shoulder at Bryony as she marches up behind their ma's wide haunches, bent double as she rips brambles from the earth. 'Tell us the story while we dig, Ma,' Gertrude says. 'We're eager for the lesson.'

Bryony gives her a shove that makes her stagger as they crouch and begin to turn the soil with their forks.

All those little faces, so close, I found that a strange thing. Little limbs that look so soft and harmless, at the distance their mammies tend to keep them. Little skipping feet and clapping hands. I think of them that way, or I did, when I thought of children. I'd no longing any more for my own. I spelled that out of myself so many years ago I've forgot the feel of it. But there, they are all about, you cannot go without spotting them jinking here and there, jibber-jabbering like birdies. I see the life in them. I seen the big ones, half child half man, and the mischief they gets into, clobbering each other and howling up through the woods where they think nothing but rabbits spies them. But the bitty ones, who'd think they have that strength secret in their chickeny arms, who'd think there was anything but feathers in their wibble-wobble heads? I've the proof of it, here in these clotty wounds and these pulpy parts that might still be my eyes.

'Your father and me, and that Guller too, were as small then as the pair of you, and likely no better, but no worse neither. We learned our right and wrong in the school house, and my own ma and pa kept my back straight and my nose out of muck.' Shilla pauses to chuck a flint from the furrow and it chinks against the pile under the elm. 'Your father weren't so fortunate with his own family, scoundrels they were, though I didn't know it then, but he weren't a bad boy. No, we might have been starved half stupid some years and freezed out of our wits every winter, but we knew good and bad. All the children did. That's what made it such a peculiar thing, what happened.'

Shilla's face is as ruddy and broad as her red fore-arms, and just as hard-looking. Bryony can't shrink her ma down to child height in her mind, with that bristly brow and her chin that sticks forward whenever she bellows – and it's usually a bellow – at her daughters. She tries to slice into the earth in the same rhythm as Shilla's spade, to keep from being noticed and halting the story, wishing Gertrude would do the same instead of toppling about.

'There were a woman then, lived in that cottage on the far side of the woods that's a ruin now. Liked to be left alone, and with good reason, they said.'

'What was her name?' asks Gertrude, already huffing with the effort of turning the earth. She's two years older than Bryony but a head shorter, measly like the last batch bun that gets made up from a scrap of dough.

'When did your nose get so sharp?' Shilla turns and Bryony tries not to look up at the swollen blue eyes that fix on her sister, but Gertrude doesn't even slow at her digging. 'Merry. Old Merry.' Shilla returns to her spade and goes on, breathing deep. 'She had hair down to her knees that she wound up in grey knots around her ears like mouldy bannocks, and just enough teeth to get the flesh from a rabbit bone. She didn't come round near the other houses much, meaning people had a good stare when she did, and the children hid behind their mams like mice when a cat's about. Me and my brother were no better, peering out at her and whispering.'

'What did they say?' Gertrude manages between wheezes.

'The same nastiness you tiddly ones likely say about old Winfrid Plait now. That she ate mice so she needn't come down to the village for her fare. That she went about at night so as not to show that she had no shadow.'

Bryony shudders at the thought of Winfrid Plait, and the top of her head that is as bald as an egg, with just a wisp of hair floating above it. She won't keep it covered, and then she sits by that pool along the river all day, so whenever you pass by you have to pretend you're not look-ing at her head or you haven't noticed. And then when you try to think of something ordinary to say, she looks right in through the fronts of your eyes and laughs at the real thought you're having, about her head like an egg.

'We were taught better than to say such things, but we knew she were different. People stopped their gabbing when she came near. She never were invited into a house like others, nor mentioned in prayers at church. That were one place she wouldn't go near at all.'

'Witches can't go in the church,' says Gertrude. She flicks soil up into the air with her fork. 'They turn to ash-dust if they cross the threshold. Piff paff!'

I heard them coming. Thought I'd slipped up and forgot a festival day. They traipsed along, clanging and clacking. It's a parade, I thought, coming along to bless their fortune-telling ox at the waterfall, or some such nonsense. They are always on and on with their rituals, blessing this and blessing that. Shouts rang about, but nothing to prick my ear. Children's voices, little birdie squawks, they don't sound a thing to fear. I kept right on with my work. Just then it were tying up the new herbs into posies, to hang and dry. I think of them as posies, but where there'd be flowers there are the hints, the glints, of their powers. Shame I hadn't the time or the insight to use them then. A stronger one than me, a woman with the true sight, might have seen what was coming. I scratched the ashes with a stick, my forked stick for the purpose, and saw only a storm in the grate.

'Who said a word about a witch?' Shilla swings round and Bryony shrinks back, bumping Gertrude with her elbows.

'Guller did,' Gertrude replies, quick as a slap. 'He said she'd been up to mischief, upsetting folk. What is it she did, Ma?'

Bryony is watching her ma too carefully to be able to give her sister a warning pinch. On their way home, they had tried to guess the mischief, and Gertie had decided the witch must have put a curse on that Webbe boy, Verlyn, and changed his arm. He's older than them, he'd have been a bab then, Gertie had said, sounding more and more sure of herself. But Bryony knows this can't be right. Verlyn is kind, not a cursed thing.

Shilla's wide red face switches between angry and sad and something else. Her eyebrows bristle. Bryony waits for a bellow, for a palm swinging her way, but instead her ma turns and continues digging. 'Never mind what Old Merry were up to. You can call it curses, but it's too long ago to be sure of it, anyway. What's certain is that she got the wrong side of Ma Guller.'

The rhythm of Shilla's spade slicing into the ground goes on. Bryony can just hear the chicks peeping from the tree behind them, the tiny wheedling sounds, so pitiful. She thinks of mandrakes again, screams that happen only in your head. What sounds does a witch make when she is hit? Would it be a roar, or a dreadful squeal like a rabbit's when its leg is caught in a trap?

Gertrude is poking her in the bum, hissing something or other about Guller being as cock-eyed as his ma, but

Bryony bats her hand away. She wants to keep the cold blood feeling that the scream in her head is making.

'That's where things went awry. Mark it, the pair of you. If somebody does you wrong, or you find yourself bitter, or jealous, you sit back and ease your mind and puzzle a while. If you can't make head nor tail of it, you puzzle a while longer and you keep on pondering until you run out of steam. You don't go with that boiling pot in your head and start scalding others with your own stew.'

Shilla's voice is turning crackly, like there's a leaf pile in her throat and her words have set it alight. Bryony tries to unthink her bad thought, that her ma is hardly the one to be preaching about cooling down before taking trouble to a person. But this burn-hole in her ma's fierceness is curious.

'Like in that tale about the lady who pushed her sister in the river?' Gertrude pipes up, grinning at her own sister.

'That was a secret,' Bryony hisses. 'Clotha said nobody knows it.'

But Shilla nods, as if the story is familiar to her. 'Yes, like that. Only Ma Guller's failing weren't jealousy. She were just plain angry. Her carvings were the finest of all the women's in Neverness, and most folk agreed on that. When the year-turning fair came and her carving didn't win the prize, she wouldn't have it. Claimed Old Merry had played a trick, charmed the judge. Said anything she could to make it seem she hadn't lost her skill. Folk laughed and made it worse, and she boiled up and boiled up until she couldn't get quiet again. And she began talking, to any that would listen, and especially to the tiddlers because we'd swallow any old telltale story like it was. Her rage was like a new, shining thing to us. Something frightening, but you drink it up, like those ghoulish tales you hear in the bard house in winter. We listened, and with all those ears turned up at her, Ma Guller's stories got wilder, and her rage became like a spell with all of us under it. We danced like empty-headed puppets for her, just to keep in the fiery heat of it, to feel the power of her rage coursing in us.'

Shilla's voice crackles so much that with a snap it seems to break, and Bryony watches her ma take one heavy step away from the furrow and thump herself down on the heap of weed stalks beside them. She looks worn out, like all that talk of fire and rage has sucked the red out of her. She is staring at the furrow she has dug, her breathing still heavy from the work, but Bryony can tell that it is not soil she is seeing with her big round eyes.

Kelpie is mewing near me somewhere. Perhaps she has found her brother. I named him after a boy I knew, once, when I were a bitty one. Hunter. By name and by nature, for he brought me a catch each night, the rascal. I called for him then.

My eyes were already blind with the blood but I could hear.
Through all their hubbub of hollering and smashing there was
the sound of his cry. Worse than the hurt I felt all through my
bones was that cry. My mind turned then, for not being able
to bear it. When I woke, it were all silent, just this mush of
me left. I am spared the sight of my Hunter, but the mewing
of his sister makes him slink through my head. She is licking
my cheek, I feel the heat of her tongue, but how it stings. Like
a lick from a nettle. Kind cat, kinder than folk. Don't mew.
Lick these crusts from my eyes, let's see what's left of them.

Bryony has an urge then, to sit beside her ma and lean
on the hillock of her shoulder, but there is a kind of
spell cast even now. Gertrude stands still beside her,
trying to quiet her gusts of breath, watching the thunder pass through their ma's face.

'We did her bidding. We followed the force of her
will, out of the village and through the wood, so strong
it was I believe our own souls were left behind. She
wished Old Merry dead, did Ma Guller. And she got
her way, with not a drop of blood on her hands.'

Shilla sits, her eyes covered by her great, grimy fingers,
and her daughters listen to the small green leaves of
the wych elm, hush-hushing above them, and the tiny
cheeps from the nest in its branches.

Their ma speaks again, as if she hears the questions
bursting in her daughters' mouths. 'Sticks, they used, that

were laying about. Stones from the crumbling cottage wall. There were such a number of us, mad with that woman's rage, we filled the house like a starling storm. After, the place were so stained, in Old Merry's blood and her howls, and in the minds of all of us, that they burned it. Old Merry were still inside. No man checked for breath, for a stirring of life, before they piled up the sticks all round and put a flame to the thatch.'

The flutter of the green leaves turns to the licking of flames in the fast hill winds. The calls of the baby birds become the mewing of a lonely cat – for a witch always has a cat – as it watches its home become a bonfire. Bryony shudders again, seeing at the centre of the bonfire the messy, sticky bundle of Old Merry, clawing away the embers of thatch that drop on to her broken body. She feels a hard nudge from Gertrude, and as the smoke and flames clear from her eyes there is the shape of her pa, stamping across the muddy ground towards them.

'What's this? Shilla? Girls, what troubles your mother?' There are little shakes running through Shilla's shoulders, her huge hands cover all of her face. Pa's shadow looms over her as his stare slides from one daughter to the other. 'What have you done, you weasels?' He lunges towards them, Gertrude swerves and he grabs Bryony by the scruff of her neck, snagging her skin so she gasps. She feels her feet lift off the ground, the fork drop from her fingers.

'Let her down.' Shilla's voice comes out snuffly. 'It's my doing, they've done nothing but listen.' Bryony stumbles as her feet touch the ground and she falls into the furrow, soil gritting her cheek.

'Listen? To what?' asks her pa.

'They heard a snippet today of what became of Merry Mort. I told them the rest, by way of a lesson.'

'You told them. All of it?'

'The parts that matter.'

'They're not the only ones wants a lesson.' Her pa's boots step right over Bryony and she peers up from the furrow just in time to see her ma's head sent flicking to one side by the clout of his fist.

'That tale's not for the ears of anyone living, least of all our own daughters.' He stands over Shilla, who stares at the ground. 'Not for nobody, ever. You learn that lesson and you keep it, Shilla.' As his boots thud away, Shilla's blue eyes meet Bryony's across the broken earth. Bryony stares, and for a moment it is like looking into her own eyes, like seeing another girl just like her. The girl is afraid, even more than Bryony, but most of all she is ashamed.

Bryony can't bear to look then. She closes her eyes, and listens to the tree, to its flickering leaves and the sad, sad sound of the lonely witch's cat.

WATER BULL BRIDE

THE WIND DRUMS ITS song at the door all night, a beat for the devil to dance to, leaving the prints of hooves around the house. Winfrid tugs her stitches tight to keep him out. I watch my needle dive through the weft, the stab and the give, and dream up patterns I'd never stitch, secret rhythms. Crosses for kisses, every girl stitches those. I've stitched my name on a ribbon and thrown it into the gorse, same as the rest. But I have a tingle under my skin for more than kisses, and there's no pattern for that.

Winfrid, my dear old Granny Win, is sewing for my wedding trunk. She plants luck into bed sheets with witching threads. She won't be drawn on the slightest thing, not the wind, not the rush of the rain on the roof. Not what's in her heart, not what's in mine. We sit here, blessed to be dry, to be warm down one side where the fire glints in my needle, while the world outside is battered to bits.

Underneath the devil's palm-beat, warping our wettened door, comes another tap tap tap. It is faster; it has blood behind it. I lift the stitching from my lap and go to listen. Tap tap tap. It is not an evil, nor an animal, noise. I catch the door as it swings in at me and there in the welter of water and wind is a man such as I have never seen. Such hair, such skin, taut across the bones of his face, taut across his limbs. He wears only a rag wrapped round him at the hips. I think of the needle through the weft, the stab and the give.

'Shelter, please,' he says. That is all, and when I show him to the seat beside mine on the settle his head falls, just like that, into my lap.

A head is for stroking, hair as soft as waterweed, strokes as soft as I can muster. What else is there to do? All that long, lean body of him curled hard against the settle cloth, his warmth on my thighs, what would I do but stroke? The tingle grows in my fingers.

When Win comes with a cup for the stranger, the saucer rattles in her clawed old hands, but he doesn't stir. She bends to catch the growl of his breath and frowns. My hands are deep in his hair.

'Dig in,' she whispers. My dragging fingers bring up, from the depth of his hair and head and skin smell, tiny shells. They are under my nails like sand, but each with an impossible whorl inside, too tiny and too deep. I rake and harvest, hundreds of them, pinky white or crusted green, some trailing a ghost of hair behind them. I hold a palmful out to Win, but she is shaking, her eyes wet with fear.

'Water bull,' she says.

I should feel the cold of fear now, for this is the tale Win tells the most, at the bard house and here on the settle. It is the one she wields to keep me home on nights like this when the dusk falls fast, safe from the river that curls like an eel around the house, safe from the sea that churns below. The water bull, her story goes, leaps inland with the sea surf on wild nights and swims up the river, sensing souls. Then he shakes off his bullhide and hunts himself a maiden. The only way she can save herself is to cross water.

I must run for the river, Win urges, and hold my skirts tight up around me so he cannot grab at them if he follows. Gingerly she pushes a wad of wool between his head and my thighs, and I edge out from beneath his warm weight. Win has a look in her eye that says *Defy and be doomed*, and it is only this that makes me shift, for how it hurts me, of a sudden, to leave his warmth. I long to stroke the dark fuzz that covers his arms and shoulders. The smell of his hair is between my fingers, how a seal pup might smell. I want to rub my face against it and breathe deep. But Win is pushing me with uncommon strength and she hurls me out through the slapping door, into the summer storm. When I turn at the gap in the wall to rub the rain from my eyes, I see Win on the threshold, and the man's strange, wide face right there above her own wizened one.

'Run, girl!' she bellows, and I know he is coming. So I do, I lift my knees high and plunge through the mud that was the path, splattering it cold up my legs, the wind twisting my skirts so I am stumbling with it. The trees are bent low, flailing against the night clouds in the fearful gale, as I tear my way up the bank, tugging up handfuls of grass, to where the river is narrow before the pool. There's no sound beyond the roar and rattle of the wind, but I know he is following by the thrum in my belly, the sense of silver eyes on me. Surely a man of such fine-turned limbs and beast-bearing will run faster than I, weighted down as I am with water? I pant at the top of the slope, hot breath where all the rest of me is shiver. The wind whips wet; it is like being in the spitting mouth of a monster, but when I look back, there are those silver eyes, those dark shoulders gleaming with rivulets.

It's but a few steps to the river now, but he is such a sight and, as he comes closer, the thrum in me deepens. I hear the sound from his mouth, a sort of snort as wild as a bull, and that is what makes my feet move then, but I am slower and slower as in a nightmare, and when I reach the river it is swollen. There is a torrent between me and the far bank, which is nothing but a tumble of mud and roots now. I could wade in but I might be swept right away and I can hear the thrash of all that water as it falls below the rocks.

So I am standing still, staring empty-headed at the twists of currents, when I feel that brindled arm, strong and thick around my waist.

I don't struggle. His body hard against my back turns me limp, quiet. I do not fall. No, we leap. A windblown, flying leap it is, over the edge of the waterfall, plunging down towards that churning pool. The sheer cold rushes into my ears.

Underneath, swaying in the dark, he turns me easily in the currents and kisses me. It is a hard bruise of a kiss, my first. When it ends, my sigh releases the last of my bubbling breath; the last threads of heat straggle out of my limbs. After that there is no more breath, or heat, for there is no need. I can move then, not as a struggling lump of a girl tangled in muddy clothes, but as water-weeds move in the eddies of a stream. When the water bull reaches out to me, it is a kind of dance that we do, down under the waterfall, and into his cave below. I watch the dark down floating up from his skin. I stroke my fingers across the very surface of it and he shudders, and the cold that has seeped through me turns into the sweetest ache I have ever felt.

Floating like a rag she were when I found her, my poor Plum, just a shred of a girl down in that hellish black pool. How I howled, for it were too much to bear, she the orphan of parents both lost to the sea. But not a soul could hear me, so there were nothing to do but haul her out myself. Knowing what had got her I thought best to be cautious, so I tugged down on one of the hazel branches hanging above until it splintered off, and by poking it into those rags, barely daring to look as I did it, I dragged her to the bank. It took some heaving and hawing to pull her up, and what with my own weeping I didn't see at first that, halfway out onto the rocks, water burst from her mouth and her eyes bulged open. When the first retching cough came I screamed, but I got to my wits and began to pummel the water out of her. Brown and gritty it came, and she spluttered against my arm like a puppy taken food too early.

The first sign I had that the drowning had twisted her mind was when I got her upright. She turned right about and made a lurch for the pool, meaning to plunge herself back down into it. She wailed when I caught her and trapped her against me, sodden as she were and so cold she numbed my fingers. I had a task of it, herding her back down the slope, as she dug in her heels and scratched at my poor red hands all the way, shrieking to be let back. Get her home and soothed, I told myself. Warm her through like a griddle cake and she'll calm sure enough.

The fire dwindled while I rocked her before it, but I daren't let go, despite the ache in my arms, and the chill in my own sides from holding her. Those shrieks did quieten to whimpers in time, though the echo of them still rang in my ears, even as she snivelled and gave in. We rocked and rocked until her breathing turned to long sleeping draughts, and I let the weight of her drop gently against the rug. I folded it up around her like a pastry pie and watched her then, stoking the fire, until dawn came white at the window.

Nobody comes back from a wallow with a water bull. At least I never heard of it. It's so rare to see one up and out of the sea, and the hunger that draws them is so fierce. It's hunger for a soul. You can know that by the tatter that's left behind.

It were still the cloths for her wedding trunk I worked at, on the stool beside her bed, though that were perhaps useless toil now. I couldn't let the patterns lie unfinished, but in my mind I planned other threadways, weaves that would wind her safe inside my house, stitches to keep man and beast at bay. I'd failed my own daughter in that way. But I would keep my granddaughter safe, whatever the burden upon me, whatever wiles it might take.

Once, while I sat at my work, Plum in her fever opened her eyes and, seeming to see what I were at, asked for a wedding dress of waterweeds.

Winfrid stitches blessings into her broideries, but she can stitch curses too. This is why my water bull does not come here to fetch me home. Some net of hers keeps him away, cast over the house like sticky cobweb.

While she has me knotted up in her spell-soaked sheets, there comes another rat-a-tip-tap at the door. This one has Linnet Lundren behind it, with her butter-silk hair and her summer-brown legs, which she crosses neat in the seat beside my bed as she smooths her frock, all proper. Win smiles at Linnet as she closes the door on us, and I look snakes at Linnet as she smiles back.

'Oh, you poor Plum, poor Plum pudding,' she sings, loud so Win will hear, while she pinches my elbow with her hot fingers. She looks at me, all over, even though I'm swaddled up in layers of linen.

'What was it like, Plum?' Linnet whispers. She does that corn-dolly smile. Last time I saw her do it was two nights before the storm, before my water bull came for me. We were all gathered in the wool-stunk room of the bard house, while Quayle the fiddler scraped on and on, waiting for a teller to take the stage. The place was full of the shrivelled ears and soft-boiled heads of all the old folk, listening like they'd never heard those tunes before. I saw Linnet with Madden Lightfoot in the corner, and I sat down right by her. I hid the snakes in my eyes for once and was the sweetest Plum pudding to her, as if we'd be friends. I got my way. While the tune droned on, Linnet turned away from Madden and whispered in my ear instead. She took my hand and drew me out to the lane to play at Threads.

The Love Hart Oak is on the bank beyond the lane, and there was Dally Oxley and his brother Pie, scuffling in the mud, the one pushing the other's face to grate against the oak trunk, but when Linnet called their names and giggled in her golden way that makes me want to hiss, they hauled up straight and showed their faces serious. Even now they've grown taller they're neither of them princes, not even handsome woodsmen who might fell a forest for a maiden, or slay a wolf for love. But Pie works in the stables sometimes, and I'd seen him thundering along the shore on the farmer's colt, at a gallop against the wind, flying, and I'd dreamt of it often after.

In my dreams before there were only those stitched-on kisses, lips pressed but not bitten, sighs with no soul behind. Even when I used to play the gorse game with the others, I got only a useless peck from Sandy Rincepan. Now I wanted a proper kiss, wet and warm, and I knew to get one I must play Threads with Linnet.

She handed the threads out, there under the Love Hart Oak, and 'hup!' she cried, and the four of us flicked up our hands. For a flash in the light I saw the threads we'd thrown and their hues as they twirled, russet, green, marigold, dun. Then Linnet swung the lantern down, holding up her skirts to make the light catch at her long brown legs, and we peered into the mud.

There was my russet crossed with Pie's dun, and Linnet's marigold twisted up with Dally's green.

'All matched!' Linnet said. 'Plum and Pie, oh, Plum Pie, the best kind! Go on,' and she nudged at me, smiling all the while at Dally, who looked like he'd won a whole summer of cream.

I stumbled out of the lantern light to the gap in the back of the Love Hart Oak. It was a struggle to get into, my dress caught on crags of bark, and I wince to remember now how I bit my lips to plump them up. How I wanted that kiss, and to smell the boy smell of stables and sweat so close and to feel so in love, for that is what I believed would happen, inside the Love Hart Oak. I waited.

'I'd rather kiss a sheepdog,' said Pie's voice through the gap, then yelled, 'I'd rather kiss Dally!' His boots stamped back down the bank and Linnet squealed as if at a good hard pinch and I heard Pie say, 'When'll I get my turn with you, Linnet Lundren? Dally might've got the face but I got the way with my hands.'

Linnet screamed and laughed and I don't know where it was they all ran to, since I stayed in the oak a very long time.

All this I remember with Linnet at my bedside.

'What was it like, Plum, Plum pudding?' she asks me again, sly, and she pinches my elbow again, and this time I don't hide the snakes in my eyes. Because corn-dolly Linnet shall never know what it is to love a water bull. Cross-stitch kisses and the Love Hart Oak and the gorse game are for sillies. Trunks of sheets and frill-edged gowns are for daft-headed maidens. They are broidered burdens, for marriage is not love. A stable-boy husband, stinking of horse dung, a hearth rolling with babs, that is not love. Love is a dance with a water bull, it is the pleasure that poured from his fingers into me.

Win may be keeping my water bull out with her stitches, but she'll not keep me in. For three days the thrum he set drumming in me has grown faster, deeper, and louder than my own heartbeat. It tells me what to do.

I put it down to the nightmares that must shadow the mind of any half-drowned person, but Plum looked blank at me from her bed when I spoke of that cursed night, trying to nudge out the truth. She'd tell not a word of the dreadful chase nor how he got hold of her, how he plunged her down, but those that have come so close to death often forget.

I spin a fine tale as I spin my yarn, and nothing goes better with broidery than stitching out a story, so Plum's been well fed with warnings. There's a tale for every kind of trouble, and the water bull tale I've told more nights than any other since Plum's been old enough to listen. I were readying my old bones to stand and tell that very tale when she went creeping out of the bard house, the night before the storm got up. She thinks I don't see but she's threaded tight to my heart and I felt the ache in my ribs before I saw the empty place she'd left, off to make mischief.

Three days I brought possets to her pillowside and kept my patience, with not a word nor a sob from her. She lay, making knots of her hair around her fingers, and when I went to smooth the sheets those tiny shells, smaller than mustard seeds, lodged in the creases of my palm.

When Linnet Lundren came I were glad to see a friend, come to make whatever mild chatter those little birds do between themselves. And it did seem to lift her soul, for right upon Linnet's leaving, Plum asked me, sweet as strawberries, 'May I have a clean dress on, Win? I've a longing to step outside and smell the sea. Can you find me one out of your chest and we'll go together?' It were nearing dusk, but so daft with joy I were to see the light back in her dark eyes, I clambered right up the loft ladder thinking of just the woollen dress to keep her warm. I were elbow-deep in the clothes chest, up there under the eaves, when I heard the creak and turned to see the ladder were tipped away.

I leave Win's howls and the house behind, following the eel bend of the river downstream for the sake of the damp water air that hangs there, to feel it soak into my skin, to make my eyes as dark as the deepest pool.

I walk past the other waterfall, where I used to beg fates from the fortune-telling ox, but I know my fortune now, and it is with my water bull. I go on, down a path hidden in blackthorn that drags its fingers through my hair and brings the grey dusk down closer. The Oxley house is at the wood's edge. I can hear the thwack and chuck of splitting logs. As the path spreads open into the Oxleys' clearing, there is not Pie but Dally, the axe high above his head, a grimace on his face as he brings it down – *crack*.

I snake my hair between my fingers. I've only my nightdress on, so I am white as a ghost girl in the twilight as I walk towards him. His lips purse as he looks at me all over, but with no linen swaddles to hide me now. Like ivy, I wind my arm around his. Like ivy, I twine myself about him. His heart thumps against my breast. The axe thuds to the ground.

It is not like diving with my water bull. I have to push Dally down to lie with me, and my breath does not turn to water nor my veins to pulsing weeds. What my body is for, what I and my water bull know so sure, Dally does not know after all, and I am sorry for him. His look when I up from our bed of leaves is as startled as when I crossed the clearing all white in the dim, and that is because I have shown him something that butter silk Linnet never could.

My nightdress is smirched but I am warm as I walk away from Dally through the trees. I am not afraid of the dark. There's no light in my water bull's secret cave. When the creepers brush and tease at me, I think of weeds and currents, and it is not far at all to the other edge of the wood and the ale room lights.

The ale room glows between the forest and the shore, and I hear the tumble of voices, and the wheeling notes of Quayle's fiddle within, as I sail right past and down on to the sand. The sea hushes so gently, and the stars make it like milk so fresh it still foams, so I step into the foam of it and crouch to wash myself. The cold tingles me, and the fiddle song from the ale room curls in my ears, and I long so for my water bull, who swam from this sea so far up the river for me. I think perhaps he will taste me in the water, so I wash and swash and wait for that arm around my waist. There is nothing, just lap-lapping waves, the sad fiddle tune and the woodsy wind from the shore.

The wind brings me louder voices, the ale room hurly grows behind me and there is laughter, the clank of cups. It's all lads in there, under Ma Prowd's owl eye. I remember Ma Prowd's brothers, Trick and Robin, both tall and one of them broad as an ox. I've seen them fight in the ale room. I begin to pick my way back over the dunes, thinking of those big, wrestling bodies, their sweating backs. The door of the ale room swings open, with a roar and a slice of lamplight from inside, and then there's three lads out, sitting on the barrels by the ale room wall. They don't see me in the black beyond the ale room glow. Neither is Trick or Robin, but one of them is Dally Oxley. He must have followed me. This makes me smile, and I am still smiling as I walk towards them. I am close enough to smell the beer steaming off them, when one of them looks up and then jumps backwards, falling right over his barrel. How easy it is.

'I told you,' says Dally. 'See? Right by the house, she were.'

I don't look at him. I stare right at the other lad who is staring back at me. It's Sandy Rincepan. He used to be a tub of a boy, but it's true he's become brown and sturdy as a dray horse. I'll give him another chance, I think. I reach out a hand and stroke his cheek. I let my hand rest on his neck.

'You'll get your fill of kisses now, Sandy,' Dally says. He grabs the other lad by the collar and they shove back through the ale room door.

We sink behind the barrels, Sandy and I. He's more of a thrust to him than Dally, it is closer to the thrum the water bull makes in me, but he whimpers like a pup and I laugh at him and push myself back up to the barrel top. 'I shall have a bull of a man,' I whisper down at him as he tries to button his trews, and I am still laughing as he thumps through the door after Dally.

The thrum has left me wanting my water bull, not these fumbling boys, and I think I will go back to the sea, and swim and swim until I find him, when out of the ale room slams a huge hulk of a man. Before I can see his face, the grip of his giant hands is around my thighs and I am slung over his shoulder like a sack. He begins to run in great shuddering strides that bump my head against his back, and he smells of sod and malt and sweat.

Dally's voice flies after us, 'Leave her be, Trick. She's only a chicken-head girlie,' but we go on, turning up the path to follow the eel-river bend. Soon we are passing right by the back of Winfrid's cottage, and I think of her trapped up there under the eaves, but when I cry out the man clamps a stinking palm across my mouth.

'Find us a secret place, shall we?' he says. His breath is heavy. 'Safe from eyes and ears.' I kick at his chest and he thwacks me across my back so hard it takes the breath from me. I gasp and gasp and a thick darkness comes over my eyes, but I can hear him saying, 'You like that, girlie? I like the sound of you liking,' and when my breath starts to come easier he thwacks me again.

I see nothing any more, but I hear the waterfall and know he has followed the river right up to the pool. My back hits the root-knotted ground. I try to look up, but he is only a shadow against the speckled sky, and the stars blur like snowflakes when he pulls my nightdress up over my head. I do cry out when he digs into me, but he turns me over and digs in again while my mouth fills with grit and leaves.

'Let me hear you liking,' he says, and he whacks my back once more.

As I gasp, the waterfall gasps above us, and my mind goes back to the leap, the dive that took my breath away and left no need for it, only the water and my water bull. It is my water bull's brindled arm that lifts me up now, that catches me close against his smooth skin, his seal-pup smell. It is his gentle beast strength that carries me to the pool's edge and his dive that saves me, plunging into deep water. No need for breath down here, my love. He wraps me in weeds and kisses me and we float in a dance, his arms about me, back to our home in the cave.

All night long I were trapped, frantic as a mouse in that wind-raddled loft, too afraid to jump lest I crack a bone, soon too hoarse to shout any more for help. As the dark sank down and my spirits with it, I begged for Plum to be safe and her mind put back rightways. How I knotted myself up that night, how my bones ached with the tearing of my Plum away from me. I wept myself ragged and as I lay close under the thatch edge, staring out at the prickle of stars, I believe I saw visions: a man as big as a water bull tramped along the river path, a sack on his back that my mind's eye made into Plum. I shook such dreads away, fearing I'd be mad by morning.

When dawn did come, I were shivering, though the clothes chest stood right beside me. I'd not the courage in my heart to look at dresses made for my lost girl. Then I heard steps on the path, a thump at the door, and I remembered Ivy Rincepan would be round for her eggs. With strength from somewhere I'll never fathom I stamped and yelled, and Ivy Rincepan pushed the door and saw the ladder and soon had me down, though my poor numb feet slipped on every rung. I didn't stop, but shouted my thanks as I ran away and up the dew-sodden bank and through the dripping trees to the waterfall.

Her night dress floated like milk curds in the pool. The prints of her little bare feet lay in the mud. Down and down I stared into that dark water, searching for bubbles, for breath, for a hint of her, but there was nothing.

Day in, day out, I sit by the pool, watching and waiting for my sweet Plum to come back to me. And while I wait, I fish up the weeds that wave in the currents here. I put my stitches to the only use I can and I'm sewing her a weed wedding dress. I float it in the shallows to keep it soft, and so that she might see it. From time to time I add green weed ribbons, to make it prettier, pretty enough for a water bull bride.

SWIRLING CLEFT

GAD WATCHES AS SIL crawls across the floor, clutching the newborn baby with one arm. She huffs out raggedy breaths and her knees scrape the boards. Her eyes are fixed on the chest in the corner. She heaves and capsizes, rolling on to her side.

'You'll have to help, Gad,' she pants. 'Get the fire tongs.'

There's no reason for her mother to need the fire tongs now. But there has been no reason for anything the last few hours – Sil's curses, Father leaving in a storm for the ale room, this blue, wrinkled thing bursting from her mother – so Gad obeys. She runs back up the stairs and holds the heavy iron tongs out to Sil.

'Open the chest. Box at the bottom.'

From under heaps of the woollen blankets and shawls that Sil is constantly knitting, Gad hauls out the box, black and cracked like an old boot. She brings it and places it beside her mother, but her hands are taken up with the shrivelled baby.

'Use the tongs.'

Gad flicks up the lid. Inside is something grey, swirling, like cobweb in a draught.

Her mother is nodding, her grimace gone for a moment. 'Gently now.'

Gad dips in the tongs and lifts them. The shred of grey web that trails from them is light as air. It brings a chill into the room. Strands of it swirl up towards her face. Sil stretches out a finger to hook it, and with a curl of her arm has it wrapped around the baby. She sighs and shifts on to her back. The shawl of cloud rolls and settles over the baby on her chest.

Gad's mother is not from Neverness. Gad's father was born on the island, and he is just as craggy and windswept, but Sil is different. She does not smell quite the same as anything else. In their house, there are warm smells, burned porridge and sheep's wool and chimney soot, and there are cold smells, like Father's rainy boots, and muddy flagstones, and sodden thatch. Wherever Sil has been, though, there is a trace of seaweed in the air, of salt sea-fog and the insides of shells.

When Gad asks where her mother grew up, Sil only says 'not here', and slams down a pot or shuts a door too fast.

Sil is not even her real name. It's the one Gad's father gave her. Sil for her silvery hair. Sil for her silky skin.

'A nickname?' Gad asked when she learned the word.

'You could say that.'

Sometimes, it is hard to see what her mother means. Sometimes, it is hard to see her mother at all. Sil is able to drift quietly out of the house without anyone noticing, and slide back in hours or even days later, leaving clammy footprints on the floor. When the sea breathes up a good thick mist like a fisher hoiking his pipe smoke and the islanders all swaddle themselves against the chill, Sil's eyes grow bright. Gad follows her out into the clogged-up world and shivers while Sil slings her hammock made of fishnet between the two hornbeam trees on the ridge. She climbs inside it and vanishes, her silveriness lost in the swirling white.

The baby, whose first blanket was that chilly wreath, turns from blue to a kind of whimpery grey. It is not the pink, bright-eyed thing Gad hoped for. When Gad first learned she would be a big sister, she had bragged to her friend, May, who had no siblings either. They used to play at sisters, pretending to be the Lightfoot girls. Gad would be Madden Lightfoot, because she was eldest, and she would pretend to teach May, as Clotha, to ride a horse, scolding her when she did not keep up with her own galloping. 'Now, I'll be the real big sister,' Gad had said, while they sat in the hornbeam together. 'I'll play with my own little sister instead.' But Gad has not played with the baby yet. It leaves damp patches where Sil lays it down. When it is not screaming, it never gurgles, only whines. Its tiny star hands that reach out, and its curled-up feet, smell of sand after it has rained.

Gad's father has not taken to it either. He took one look when he reeled in from the ale room, and said to Sil, 'I suppose you'll be off, then.' When Sil didn't answer, he mumbled something about taking the flock to higher ground. Gad has not seen him since. When she asked where the higher ground was, Sil only said, 'A long walk,' and went back to hushing her squally bundle.

Gad spies on her mother and the baby through the split in the bedroom door. Sil is sick, grey and puffy like she gets when the weather's too warm, only worse. She wedges herself in the window seat with the casement wide open, so autumn leaves fly in. Even the air on Gad's eye is cold. The baby only stops screaming when Sil digs that weird piece of cold smoke out of the chest and lets it spread over the baby's head.

'Did you cover me with the cobweb when I was small?' Gad asks, bringing in the cold water Sil asked for.

'It's not cobweb.'

'What is it then?'

But Sil is choosing not to listen. She sits with her feet in the water bowl, her eyes closed, breathing in deep, deeper, as if air is not enough.

As she often does when her mother is drifting off, indistinct, Gad wedges the door to her room shut and wriggles into the dusty shadow under her bed. Shoved into the darkest corner is the old hamper, its weave broken and spiky. She undoes the impossible knot she made up herself to keep it shut, and feels inside. In the hamper, Gad has gathered proof that Sil has been here, being her mother, for nearly eight years now. That is almost all of Gad's life.

Gad is not silvery and silky like her mother. She has the same swarthy skin and straw-tuft hair as Father, and the same distrust that Sil will stay. Her father's question echoes: 'I suppose you'll be off.' She doesn't know why he said it, then, with the baby coughing against Sil's breast. She does know that Sil was not always here. She thinks she remembers the first time Sil's arms folded around her, the chill that seeped from her skin. If there was a different mother before that, when Gad was as small as the creaky baby is now, then she must have gone and not come back. Her friend May has always had the same mother, with the same dark eyes as her. Gad has never told May that Sil is not wholly hers.

Each time Sil is gone from the house, Gad searches out something to prove that she is real, and hides it in the hamper. There is the cup on a long piece of string, which Sil tied to Gad when she was little in case it tumbled from her pudgy hands. There is the head of a doll they made together, the straw body rotted away. Mostly, there are things Sil has knitted with the wool from Father's sheep: a sock, a bonnet, an unfinished mitten.

With her hand in the basket, Gad touches each little piece of Sil. She can't be sure it wasn't Father who made the string cup. Perhaps even the doll was his idea. But that cold smoky thing, the cobweb, is somehow entirely Sil. If Gad can just know what it is, if she can hold it, have it, she will be more sure of her mother.

Gad creeps to her mother's bedroom door. She waits for the draught to grow colder and the baby to settle, its breath like raking tides under Sil's sighs. Then she sneaks in, to the crib, scoops the cobweb shawl under her arm and runs as quietly and as quickly as she can, out of the house, along the hill crest. As she runs, aiming for the first hornbeam, she stuffs the cold cobweb inside her dress. It clings to her skin, and by the time she is climbing the tree she can feel wetness against her chest.

She wedges herself on a knobbly branch and peers inside her dress. There is nothing left but a damp patch, a greyish stain. The baby's cries rattle from the house, growing louder, and she hears Sil yelling her name. Gad puts her hands over her ears.

'What have you done, Gad?' Sil shouts.

The wind through her wet dress is making Gad shiver, and her mother's angry voice sends the chill deeper.

'Gad. Get back here.'

She slides from the branch and drops hard to the ground. Her feet ache with the thump.

Inside, Sil beckons her into the bedroom. Her face is smudgy with wet, as grey as a raincloud. She looks at Gad's damp dress and closes her eyes.

'That was my last scrap.'

'Scrap of what? What is it?' Gad says.

'We're going to get more. You'll have to help.'

Gad crosses her arms. But the baby's coughs are so pitiful and her mother's face so strange and blurry, she cannot refuse. When Sil stands, Gad lets her lean on her shoulder.

'Take those,' Sil says, kicking at the fire tongs that still lie on the floor. Gad feels her mother wince with each step as they leave the house.

Sil has soaked a cloth in the water bowl and swaddled the baby to her chest. Gad can hear its dry croaks, a frog too far from a pond. They take the path down the seaward side of the hill, where the bare trees are bent from the wind that hurdles the high cliffs below. They have never been this way together.

The high cliff drop is one reason Gad is not supposed to come this way, but she is allowed to follow the gorse-maze paths on the headland, which is just as high. The real peril on this side of the hill, she knows, is the Cleft. There are five Clefts around the pleated edge of their island, deep furrows that begin high up where the hill moss is dry and cut down through rock to the sea. Rain water from the crags trickles down them, but trees also slide and sheep crash down their steep sides. All are forbidden to Gad. Each has a tale of woe, told at the bard house, meant to keep children and fools away. One has a drowned tower in the sea at its mouth, which has gold buried in it but also a dreadful curse. Another is where folk say a water bull comes up from the sea and steals pretty girls away. Each has a name that sends prickles of curiosity over Gad's scalp. Riddling, Hurling, Scowling, Humbling; the one below them now, as they skid down the hillside, is Swirling. In the tale about Swirling Cleft, it is clogged with a mist so thick that it drowns fool-hardy wanderers.

Sil is walking slower and slower, the weight of her arm heavier across Gad's shoulders. She comes to a halt and leans against a crooked tree.

'No further,' Sil whispers. She is swaying in the wind. 'You'll have to go. The two of you.'

'I don't know where we are going.'

Sil points down the slope.

'But Father says never to go there.'

Sil is already unwrapping the cloth from her body. She kisses the baby's ashen cheeks. Envy twists in Gad's throat.

'If you won't go it'll be the end, Gad, for the poor mite.'

Now that she is being ordered into Swirling Cleft, the warning tales seem more real. She pictures herself tripping on bones, drowning in fog, falling. Sil reties the swaddle cloth on to Gad so the baby is pressed against her chest. It is not only the wet cloth that chills her.

'If you fall, fall backwards,' Sil says. 'Go right to the bottom. Bring as much as you can. Use the tongs.' She tugs Gad's hand to her for a moment and then gives her a little push towards the path. 'I'll wait.'

Sil's face is hard and weary. Gad does not dare to say no. She lets her feet carry her, faster as the path steepens, until she slithers to a halt and looks down at the swags of mist that hang heavy in the throat of Swirling Cleft. She cannot see Sil any more. The baby's creaking cries wind around her ears. Gad takes a gulp of grassy air, and steps down into the grey.

The mist films her face. Gad swipes it away and watches it roll up like loose sheep's wool, making a cave around her head. By sweeping her arms as if she is swimming, she keeps a space ahead of her to breathe. Wispy trails flow from her hands.

The mist is stickier and colder as she goes lower into Swirling Cleft. It creeps into her ears and muffles her footsteps. She cannot tell if she is stepping on moss, or stone, or sand. Down and down she goes, on an endless hidden staircase. Her skin is wet where the mist has touched her, and she is shuddering with cold when she feels the path narrow to nothing beneath her feet. She cannot clear enough mist to see what is below her. Gritting her teeth, she turns around and slithers feet first. She finds footholds in rock and ivy, and grips with arms stretched around the rasping baby, trying not to drop the tongs.

She hears the hiss and hush of the sea behind her, and when her feet finally land on sand and she turns, there it is. She has come right to the bottom of Swirling Cleft. The air here is bright beneath the cloud. There is a sparkle in the grey sand, and in the pushing, tugging waves.

Ropes of the thick mist hang down like tangled creeper over the ledge she has climbed. Coils of it lie on the rocks. The baby on Gad's chest is no longer crying, only breathing the soft sighs of sleep. She walks around the edge of the grey cove. Where the ivy reaches down over the rocks, its leaves are white. She finds festoons of thick, deep mist hung there like her mother's hammock, and mounds of mist like grey clothes dropped on the floor.

Gad unwraps the baby and lowers it into one of the hammocks. It opens its eyes and gurgles at her. When Gad holds out a finger for its tiny ones to grasp, the baby smiles. It looks more like it should. The baby does not get wet where the mist touches it, but rolls happily as if it were in fleece. Sil would love it here, Gad thinks. She would be at home. Gad lets this thought fill her with a silvery shiver.

Beyond the hammocks, Gad sees a mist curtain hanging. She leaves the baby and goes for a closer look. It seems to cover the opening of a cave, and she is about to push it aside when she hears a soft clack-clacking sound from within. She knows that sound. She tries to think, her head fuzzed with the hazy air. It is the same sound her mother's needles make when she knits, but fainter, like bubbles breaking water. She hears a voice singing, a glimmery echo in the cave like the sea in a shell. The song is one she has heard Sil sing, to her when she was small, and to the baby. She thinks of her mother up there on the windy hill, the scrap of mist she stole from her. The singing and the gentle clacking soothe her, and she sits on the grey sand with her back against the rock, listening, drifting.

Gad wakes with a start. She leaps up at the sound of the baby's babble and goes to lift it from the hammock, its little star hands grasping at the vapour. She should not have stayed so long. But there beside the baby is a great bundle, mist that seems to be folded like soft wool garments, packed into a pile and tied up with ivy twine.

With the baby on her chest, Gad stands by the cave curtain. 'Thank you,' she whispers, not sure she wants to be heard. Then she hurries to where the white ivy hangs lowest and begins to climb, holding the bundle out with the tongs to keep it from her skin.

There is no sign of Sil on the path. Even out of the mist, Gad is juddering with a cold that has sunk right into her. The baby feels so much heavier now against her wheezing chest, but she hurries uphill, carrying the misty bundle to her mother.

When she reaches the house, she finds Sil by an open window, her feet in the water bowl. She blinks at Gad for a few moments, and then with a gasp leans and wraps her arms around her. Gad buries her shivers deep in her mother's chilly hug.

As Sil unwraps the baby and takes the bundle, Gad sees she has laid fleeces and blankets in the armchair, making a woolly nest.

'Get warm,' Sil says, guiding her to the chair. She tucks Gad into the sheepskins and folds over layers of knitting, then kisses Gad's knees through the wool.

Gad's chills begin to ebb away. She watches Sil untie the bundle and wrap herself and the baby in the hazy garments. Sil smiles at Gad from her own misty nest in the window seat.

'Why don't you live there?' Gad asks after a while. Her mother has been dozing with the baby at her breast.

'Where?'

'Swirling Cleft.'

'Because of you,' Sil says.

Gad's cheeks are the warmest part of her.

'Your father,' Sil says, peering out of the window as if he might be right there, back from the higher ground. 'He had you on his back when he came down the Cleft one day, following some foolish sheep. You were a little thing, wailing to break a heart. I watched him while he kept searching, you crying all the while.' She shifts the baby in her arms, but keeps her sleepy eyes on Gad. 'I followed him, listening to you, all the way here.'

'But you stayed?'

'Babs need mothers. You needed me. Your father, well, he needed me too. Are you warm now?'

Gad nods. Sil wriggles deeper in her cloudy heap. Through the window behind her, Gad sees the mist rolling in. She feels the chill drift in the room, but she is warm, wrapped in the wool of Sil's knitting. She breathes in the salty fog scent and watches the baby stretch its star hands to grasp at the swirling mist.

THUNDER CRACKS

I'VE HEARD IT SAID, a strong wind can send a
man's mind sailing out of his head. It's that way with
horses. Perhaps a storm, the kind that shifts trees and
blows out new caves, can do worse. A storm like we had,
that autumn, might be enough to possess a person. It
might send a girl's sense skittering out of her head and
leave only thunder in its place. That would be one story.
But I said I wouldn't tell. I promised, and I've kept it.
Nothing good would come of it, for folk would take the
tale their own way. Madden Lightfoot, my young stable
hand, calm as can be now with the horses. Taken up
where her father left off, so sudden.

I said I wouldn't tell, but I'd like to ask her, 'Do you
remember, Madden? Or was it the thunder got in your
head?'

At noon, while Madden and her father Pike were at work on the Prowds' High Farm, the sky had turned to twilight, and the storm rolled in. By the time they had trudged down from the farm, the lower slopes and lanes were pouring new rivers to meet the gnashing sea. Madden shuddered at the might of the water, at the wind that urged her towards it. All through that twilit day, the west wind rampaged, hurling curds of sodden sky against the earth, soaking it through.

All night, Madden, her little sister Clotha, her ma and father stayed awake, to watch the roof in case it should slip, to watch for water seeping through the walls. The storm filled them with a kind of fearful glee, and they did not think of resting.

Now, after another day shut up in the house, Madden is dulled by the lack of sleep, but restless still, the throb the wind left in her matching the storm outside. It is dusk, but there is no light to fade away. There have been no shadows today. The roar that still echoes around the house is lulling. Clotha has given up poking at her sister with her bony feet.

All day their ma has flitted in and out to help neighbours scoop belongings from the torrent in the village below, or tie down the ones that might blow away. The gossip is that the waves have turned to monsters of scum and broken fish, and have churned the shore up so the rocks, when they can be glimpsed, are all in the wrong places. Madden longs to see this, to feel the sea's wrecking strength.

It is not only the shore that the storm has whipped cock-eyed. With the earth turned to loose mud, trees have begun to slide. The copse at the river bend is bunched together at the bank, her ma said, and soon the trees will slither into the torrent one by one, like reluctant horses into a ford. This Madden also wants to see. Even Galushen's great oak, her ma told with a gleam in her eye, has fallen and clipped off the chimneys from his huge house. 'Picture the look on his snooty wife's face,' Ma grinned. 'We're all the same in the eye of a storm.'

The sight of the headland, though, Madden is glad to be spared. Only a week ago, the villagers burned the gorse, and her ma told how the rain has washed the soot right down the rocks, turning the whole headland black. Madden had not been there for the burning, for she still mourned Crab Skerry, lost forever in the gorse fire of four whole years ago. Her memory of him is secret, like the kiss she never gave.

Clotha has relished these snippets of storm news, jinking about the house like a restless dog, pressing her ear to walls, holding out her hand as if hoping for drips through the roof. Madden stays curled in a chair. She cannot even hear the sea beyond the roar and smash of wind and rain, but she wants to crawl into the cave at the far shore end, and find what new passageways have opened and shut now. Her father showed her this cave, a hiding place that is never the same twice. He used to take her there, while her ma was still nursing Clotha, and send her in while he kept an eye on the tide.

'What did you find?' he would ask when she came out, blinking, and he would make her draw the cave's shape in the sand, showing how it had changed since the last time. Then one day, after a wild spring tide, when the shape she drew in the sand showed a cavern that had never been there before, he sent her back in. 'Wait,' he said, 'until you can see in the dark.'

She had crouched in the nook of rock, hearing her breath echo, until there on the cavern wall, she saw. It was the shape of a horse, and a boy leading it. Small, but not a trick of the rock: carved in. Then her father was there, at her shoulder.

'Shift,' he whispered, pulling a chisel from his pocket. She watched him chip around the boy's head, the stone ringing with each hammer knock. 'Come and look.'

Now it was a girl who led the horse across the cavern wall, with long curling hair like her own.

'Soon as you're old enough,' her father said, 'we'll get you as skilled with the horses as any boy. And if time comes I'm gone, you'll have my work, and take care of your ma and Clotha.'

Now, Madden pictures the sea churning sand through the cave, washing it away, so that the cavern is opened up again, the horse and girl showing on the wall. Then she watches the fierce water scrubbing them out.

'Stay awake,' Clotha hisses in her ear, pinching her arm. Madden rubs her eyes, hearing again the storm roar that had faded for a moment. She must not sleep.

Clotha is hunting for drips again, but it is not the roof that worries Madden.

Her belly had turned to ice that day in the cave, for horses terrified her even then. Now, at sixteen years old, she's been apprenticed four years at the High Farm, where her father makes workers of the wild horses and knocks the farm-born ones into shape. Not the son he wanted, but his eldest child, and he has no inkling how hard she has to try not to run away from those beasts, to be still when she looks at their rolling eyes, their twitching shoulders. She cannot harness their might, the way her father does.

Instead, she dreams of horses every night, the thunder of hooves rolling towards her, and she thrashes awake just as she will be trampled. But worse than the terrors: ever since the gorse-burning when Crab was lost, she has begun to wander in her sleep again. She has not done this since she was a child.

Only last week, Robin Prowd, the lanky, straggle-haired man who gives her father work at the High Farm, was waiting at the gate one morning.

'A word, in the house, Pike,' he said. When her father came back out his cheeks were as red as embers.

'See this?' Pike pointed to where the heavy iron bar, the one for keeping the barn door shut and the horses in, lay on the ground. 'Seeing as you took it down, you put it back up now.'

Madden stared. The bar was as long as she was. 'I can't,' she said.

'You did, so you will. The colt's out and the mare too.'

After she'd struggled with the weight of it long enough to sweat, burning with a disgrace that didn't seem to belong to her, he had taken one end and dragged it away. 'If those horses don't come back, if we can't find them ourselves, we'll bear the cost. Robin saw you do it himself, middle of last night.'

She didn't believe him, but climbing into bed that night, she found the mud on her sheets. Then the shame she had not felt for years came sidling back.

When she was young, her ma would coddle her. 'He's worried for you, that's all,' she used to say, while Pike shook his head. Her father's silence, his stony eyes, told her something else.

She must not sleep.

Thunder breaks again, a long cracking sound as though a piece of cloud has broken off, and somewhere nearby wood splits and creaks. The cave at the far shore end is roaring.

I said I wouldn't tell. Not this time. It bothered me bad enough that I told Pike Lightfoot his daughter had been up to the farm in the night and let out the horses. I only meant it were odd, and he should keep an eye on her. But there he stood and yelled at her with all the farmhands to hear. There'd been something strange about her that night, walking so slow but strong enough to take down the iron bar, looking at me but not looking.

Still, I'd almost forgot it when this storm came in. I'd the horses to think of, bolted after the fence gave in the night, and Trick in a rage, blaming all but himself for the loss. I've seen plenty of storms blow in, blow havoc and blow out again. It can be a fine thing, in its way, takes off a skin of earth, washes out the grumblings and stinks that have been growing, and leaves us fresh as peeled apples. But there's storms and there's storms, and this one, it were ruthless, never-ending. Enough to put thunder in anyone's head.

It were right up high on the hill I saw her, while I trudged out looking for the horses. Scrap of washing, I thought, flapping up there against a rock in the middle of Murnon's sheep field. Meant to pick it up and keep it for its owner. But when I got closer I saw it were a nightdress and, inside it, Madden Lightfoot. She lay still as if she were warming herself on a sunny spring day.

I called out, loud as I could in the wind and the sideways rain. She stirred from the rock where she'd been lying and looked up, and then she walked right off, in the opposite way from me. I shouted some more, but on she went, like she didn't hear at all. Put me in mind of how she'd been when I caught her by the barn the other night. Something not right. And I remembered that poor girl Plum, then, who went out in a rainstorm that night a while past. What trouble that led to, though

Trick never admitted his hand in it. My brother was out here, somewhere. The least I should do was to see this girl safe, so I followed.

The oddest path Madden took across Murnon's field, seeming to feel with her feet in all that mud. Then she climbed right over the field wall, even though there's a stile but a few yards away, and dropped down to go on walking on the other side. I went by the stile but I kept my eye on her. She didn't go fast, but steady in spite of that jostling wet wind. Two more fields she crossed in that way, straight over walls like she hardly noticed them.

I were wet to my guts by then, and she'd not as much as turned to look at me. I were wondering what to do, if I should make a grab for her and get her home by sheer force. But she turned into the wood, pushed her way fearless through the holly thickets and there in the gully, up to her knees in a mire of leaf and black mud, she found my mare.

It seemed a blessing that – as if she were paying me back for letting the same creature out before. I had some trouble to get my hand knotted firm in the mare's mane, get her soothed.

'Is that what you're out for, helping find my bolted horses?' I asked. She stared at me but she didn't answer. Her look seemed to go through me. 'Might be time to get home now, get dry,' I tried. I were starting to feel a dunnock, talking with no answers. But then the thunder cracked, and the poor mare whinnied, and the girl gave a shudder, and all in a rush so sudden after her standing there so quiet, she ran at me and grabbed my hand. She were yelling something all jumbled. She caught me by surprise, pulled my hand so hard I lost my grip on the mane, and dragged me away from the mare. I had a struggle, then, running after the horse in all that mulch, and Madden Lightfoot went marching off, and I couldn't catch up with her until we were halfway back over the field.

She turned and saw me. Both of us were as draggled as trolls, but that odd, empty look in her face had gone. She seemed to know me again.

'You did me a good deed,' I said. 'Let me see you home safe.'

But she looked at the mare and shook her head. 'Please don't tell my father you saw me out,' she said, and with that, she ran off, down towards her house.

Clotha's squeal is what makes Madden look down and see the muddy prints she has left. Her ankles are thick with stuck-on leaves, and her dress as brown as if it were made from a sack. But it is too late to clean up, there are voices at the door and her ma sweeps in fast behind her, head down in a whisk of water and wind. She is in a wretched state herself, her hair twizzled into a soggy nest and her bluish face scratched all over, and everything soaked.

'Where d'you get to, and get like that?' she asks, and shakes her head at Madden. 'Your father saw you coming down from the field. He'll want an answer. Now see if you can get that fire up. I'd give my fingers and toes for hot water, if I could feel them.'

Madden shoves her feet into her boots to hide the mud, just as her father follows through the door, and hurls his sopping cap on to the floor. Her mind is full of that horse, and Robin there too with her, all of a sudden in the field. She wonders what she has done this time. There's not a moment to puzzle out which would be least bad, to say she's gone wandering in her sleep, or that she'd purposely disobeyed, for already her father has his shoulder against the great oak table and is groaning with the effort as he pushes it towards the door. When he has it wedged there, he stops, and leans. 'We'll have no more of it,' is all he says.

Madden stays quiet. At least this way she cannot do it again.

'But the roof, Pike,' calls her ma, from where she is digging out dry clothes from the cupboard. 'If it slides we'll be stuck under a heap of wet thatch.'

'It can't go on much longer, this storm,' Pike replies. 'Safer in here than out there.' He doesn't even look at Madden.

'Well, I'll keep awake, even if you can't stay up another night.'

'Me too,' Madden says. She cannot shake the horse out of her head and is afraid of it becoming a whole sky full of horses, thundering into her dreams, giving her terrors. If she stays awake, she cannot dream. She cannot wander in her sleep.

Pike is the only one who climbs up to the sleeping loft, still in his wet clothes. Her ma sits Clotha between her knees by the hearth while they dig for sparks.

'What shall we sing, to keep wide awake?' Ma starts humming a rambling tune.

Behind it Madden can hear the tick, tick of the dripping thatch, drifting in and out of patterns, now like a clock, now like a patter of running feet. The room is foggy with smoke from the fire where water flicks down the chimney. She thinks of Crab, trapped in the burning, smoking gorse. Then she tries to shift her mind from that, and thinks instead of the cave at the far shore end, all the deep, dark rooms it might have now, how the girl leading the horse might have been smashed right away by the sea.

Ma's singing has turned to a burble, and now it has become only whistling snores. Clotha's head is resting on her knee, mouth open. The wind growls at the walls. Madden's eyelids are heavy, heavy as the oak table she'd never be able to shift, too heavy to hold back a cloud of horses. Around the house, thunder cracks.

Back at the stable, and the mare safe, I remember I thought on Madden Lightfoot. Couldn't make head nor tail of it. *Don't tell my father*, she'd said. But I didn't like the idea of keeping it from Pike, if she were to go wandering about again, and something were to befall her out in that storm. It was still raging then, and I'd seen on my way back up to the farm how everything were shifted about. Trees down or standing where there were none before. Lanes gone and hedges washed away and all the landmarks made so they muddled the eye, if they were there at all. It gnawed at me, the thought of her out alone with that uncanny look about her, like it were another creature behind her eyes. Trick hadn't found the colt, and he'd left for the ale room. To see our sister kept well there, he said, but I knew the reason were her liquor and not her good health. So, with another horse to find, I made up my mind it would be a good deed, to pass by the Lightfoots' and have a word with Pike.

Night had fallen by then, with scant moonlight behind the running clouds, but I made it back down to the house. I were waiting, thinking out what I'd say, when a boom of thunder shook the whole place, and then I saw the door open a crack, the glow from their fire showing. It shifted a bit more, then out she slid, Madden Lightfoot, and came walking right out into the night.

'Weather for staying indoors,' I said, or some such, as she passed near me. It were like before: she didn't seem to hear. The girl were looking at me odd again, with no meaning in her face, and then went walking right past.

I didn't like to shout, I remembered the way she'd shuddered at the mare's whinny in the wood, and grabbed at me so hard I lost my footing. I weren't afraid, quite; wary perhaps. I set out after her.

The rain were easing, but the wind still whipped at us. She didn't seem to mind it. The moon when it showed between the clouds lit her way a little, though this time she didn't make for the wood but wandered towards the village. She trotted across the river bridge without a moment's pause, though the water had torn whole trees from its banks. The village was but a mire, and the shut-up houses looked ready to sink right into it. On she went, not another soul out and about, until we'd reached the shore.

Bitter the air was there, and stinking of the fish that the sea had smashed on the rocks. All the foam on the high waves showed pale, and the sound of it enough to make a man quake, but on she went, walking where the shore-edge path used to be but were now just a mess of rocks and mangled turf. Partway along, I saw a fluttering shape crouched on the beach. It stood as we went by, and I saw that it were Guller the fowlmonger, dangling a dead cormorant from each fist. He shouted something about fine pickings, and I shuddered, but Madden did not even turn.

At the end of the shore path she began climbing up the outcrop that hangs over the cave there. I struggled on the wet rock, all covered with seaweed flung up and mud flung down, but she got up nimble as a goat and when I heaved up beside her, the sight were a wild one. I'll never forget.

The middle of the rocky ledge had crumbled right away and a spray from the cave below came puffing up out of it like smoke. Waves smashed and boomed down there, and I shouted out for her to be careful, but she paid no heed. I ran to where she was bending to look down, and above the rushing of the water I heard a panicked whinny. I could hardly make it out, but down in the cave were one of my horses, thrashing in the water. There were nothing I could do for the poor beast. I held on to the girl to keep her from falling and together we stared down.

It was then I heard a yelling behind us and there was a man, clambering up the rocks. It were Pike Lightfoot.

'Madden!' he shouted.

He were slipping on those black rocks. A mercy it would have been if he'd never got on to the outcrop.

'Watch how you step,' I called, but that only made him gather strength, and then he were standing before us. The girl didn't say a word.

'Madden!' he shouted again, but it were me he looked at. 'Give her to me.'

I wanted to tell him not to shout, not to fright her. 'I only followed her,' I said, 'to keep her safe.' I couldn't say, right there beside her, that something seemed not right. That she'd thunder in her head.

Pike were right up close, then, and nowhere to go with the hole right behind us. The wind were like a hand swiping at us. He grabbed hold of me, and the wave that must have come in below made a boom like it would blow us into the sky. The air split with it, and Madden gave a scream, and she pushed us away from her, me and Pike, with such a might that we both fell. I smacked the rock, but Pike, one quick tumble and he were gone.

I looked down into the cave but I could see nothing, only the swirl of that treacherous water.

Some while I crouched there, between that staring girl, with her strange, quiet face, and the roaring from the cave. Whichever horse of mine had been down there had gone, and so had Pike Lightfoot. I were looking down again, when I felt her hand on my shoulder. She gazed about at the rock and the shore below, all those big, churning waves, and I saw her eyes had changed to knowing again. They had fear in them now. She said to me, 'Please, Robin, don't tell my father that I went walking in the night, will you? I'll make up for the horses I let out. Please don't tell.'

She trembled like a struck bell.

'I won't tell,' I said.

And I haven't told. For what good could come of it?

Her ma is still snoring, and Clotha twitching in her sleep alongside, when Madden creeps into the house. The great oak table is shifted back from the door, and she wedges a stool against the door to keep it shut.

She will say the wind must have done it, that she woke to hear it banging in the dark. Her father will be fast asleep still up in the loft. Nobody need know that she has wandered in the night at all.

The dripping from the thatch and in the chimney has stopped. Even the wind has given up its howling and makes only weary whispers about the house.

Madden crouches beside the dwindled fire and pokes in new kindling, to make it warm for when the three sleepers awake.

EARTH IS NOT
FOR EATING

CROUCHED BETWEEN THE GREY bean plants, Iska watches her mammy drop pinches of earth into her mouth like breadcrumbs. She sits on the ground with her legs stuck out, the soles of her dirty feet showing, and as she drops and chews, she rubs her belly.

Iska has washed the cabbages for her mammy enough times to know that earth is not for eating. The sight sluices the grumble right out of her belly.

Only this morning she brought her sleeping mammy a breakfast, the last egg coddled just soft how she taught her, carried quick to the box bed so it was still warm. When Iska drew the curtain back, the wholesome scent of the egg under her mammy's nose woke her. She took one look and batted Iska away, her cheeks pulsing and her hand clapped over her mouth as she dashed for the piss-pot. Iska watched Skipper lap up the orange yolk with one slap of his long doggy tongue.

And now her mammy is swallowing earth as if it's the best of a big catch, the finest of all the fish they've not eaten for so long that Iska can't remember when it was Pa went out on the boat. It must be full by now, it must be rocking under a mountain of plump silver bodies, slithering in the heave of each wave. There between the drooping beans she thinks out the words her mammy used to say for every supper: 'Sea be calm and tide hurry fishermen home.' It's a hot day, but the cold creeps up under her ribs when she can't remember either the last time she heard her say this in her soft song voice.

This morning Iska has been waiting for Granny Turpin to come like she used to, and scold her mammy and make her get spick and span and the house too. She'd hoped Granny Turpin would stop her mammy from eating the earth, but she has hoped this for many a morning, and her granny has not arrived to bark her name at the gate.

Iska crawls backwards through the bean plants and idles through the dunes, the sand warm under her toes. She does not like to play alone in the cave at the far shore end, because there are ghosts in there, her mammy says. So, she wanders away from the shore, and up the sheep track that climbs the hill to the Rincepans' whitewashed house.

Her friend Pud is sprawled on the step in the sunshine, cracking last year's cobnuts and prising the shrivelled hearts from their shells. When Iska tells him what she's seen, Pud chews and ponders.

'Maybe make your mam a mud pie for supper, then,' he says. 'Or snail stew.'

When Pud has stopped his snigger, Iska says, 'She won't do a proper supper for me neither. I get green leaf mush, not even a fish or anything.'

Pud has a good stare at Iska's bony knees next to his own, which are like fat browned potatoes. He swallows. 'And does she look the same, or has she gone all wrinkled or ugly-faced?'

'Ugly yourself,' says Iska, and she flicks the nut she can't crack at Pud's head. But there is something odd, now she thinks, about how her mammy looks. She's getting fat as an ale man on green slime and soil. And she's not worn a Mam dress like usual, not even when Iska's old nurse, Werrity, came to visit and she hooted at her mammy draped in one of Pa's shirts.

'Remember that tale we got from your old nurse Werrity once,' Pud starts, 'about when the bab gets swapped for a fairy one that's all grisly and greedy?'

'The changeling,' says Iska.

Pud stamps his foot and crunches a nut to bits. 'You got a changeling mam.' He looks sidelong at Iska. 'Remember how she said you tell? Changeling babs are pretending, but they can't do it proper. They look dog ugly and act all wrong and they only want changeling food. If you came out of the hill where it's all mud and roots, then you'd want to eat that too.'

'That was only a story. And anyway, it was a bab, not a mammy.'

'It's not only babs. You seen Gad's ma? She's likely a changeling mam, too. Always cold and foggy like she'd rather live in a fairy hill full of mist than here. No good at pretending, neither.'

'My ma's not misty,' says Iska. 'She used to be pretty.'

'Muddy, though,' Pud says, narrowing his eyes. 'She goes off wandering about the marsh, you said, and won't let you go with her.'

'So?'

'Plenty of mud there. She must be going to see her fairy babs. 'Stead of you.'

Iska picks up a handful of cobnut shells and showers them down over Pud's brown head.

The waft of Ma Rincepan's cooking through the open door is so rich and meatily good that Iska lingers, finding as many games to play with cobnut shells as will last until Pud gets called in. All the while she thinks over what a changeling might pretend wrong. It's true that her mammy won't sing to her any more like she used to of a glowery evening with Pa home off the sea. She hardly whispers a word unless to scold. The house is so quiet that all Iska hears is Skipper whining with his nose in the grate. The worst thing was when her mammy took the hare skin and threw it in the fire. It was an old thing, worn half bald and with raggedy ears, but her mammy used to wrap her in it every night in her bed, even though she'd got so big lately it would only go around her shoulders. The hare skin smelled of her real mammy. It was the only thing in the house that didn't stink of fish and sea, and now it has gone.

She is wondering if all changelings hate fur because they love mud, when Ma Rincepan reels them in with a yell. When she spies Iska she slaps a hand on top of her head and gives her a turn right round.

'Hup to it home with you. And we'll take your poor ma a plate. She must be starved, and in her state.' Ma Rincepan has Iska's hand gripped a bit too tight in her rough red fist as she stamps along, just so fast as to make Iska run every few steps to keep up. The steam from the plate smells so good it hurts her insides and the thought of losing her morsels of meat to Skipper along with that last egg is too much to bear.

'Please, Ma Rincepan,' she says, when they have come down the hill and are passing the dunes. 'We can stop here. Mammy doesn't much like meat for now anyway.'

'Nonsense,' Ma Rincepan bellows, and there is no sign of Skipper as she bustles right through the door and into the darkened house, past the cold hearth, and creaks up close to the box bed.

When Ma Rincepan pulls the curtain open, Iska can just make out the bump of her mammy asleep in the big box bed, the sheet tucked round her neat as pastry. She looks across at her own little boat of a bed, under the eave where her wooden gull hangs, turning slowly in the draught. She takes a step closer. The bedclothes twitch and two glowing dog eyes rise up to meet her. Did her mammy put Skipper to bed in her place? As Iska glares back she feels a thought slide, cold and terrible as December sea water. Only a changeling mammy would put a dog to bed instead of a girl. Pud said they pretend wrong. They wouldn't know the difference. The changeling mammy must have kissed Skipper's wet nose and made the little boat rock and set sail, just as if it were her in there. Or would this soil and twigs and boiled leaves mammy not even know to do that?

Ma Rincepan lets her take the warm plate and creep back out to the garden, and while she munches the juicy meat and spludges fatty potatoes around in her mouth she can hear them murmuring inside. It makes her shudder even as she eats, that careless, muddy thing leaving soil all over her mammy's sheets.

Next day Pud finds her nestled against their favourite dune in the soft morning sun, chewing on raw beans. 'They good?' he asks, eyeing the pods scattered in the sand.

Iska winces as she swallows. Raw beans are not good at all, her throat hurts, but they were the only thing she could find in the garden that looked like food. 'You said I've got a changeling mammy,' she says, letting Pud pick the last bean from her palm.

'So?'

'She laid the dog in my bed.'

'That's bad.'

'And she's not washed a thing, not for ages. My real mammy was always wanting to wash the fish smell out of the house.'

Pud puffs himself up serious as the schoolmaster. 'And does she ever talk of your pa or wish him home to you?'

Iska shakes her head.

'Then it's certain as summer. A changeling mammy wouldn't notice the fish smell, and she wouldn't know you should even have a pa, would she? If he were already gone when she came.'

Iska tries to bite the wobble out of her lip.

'Come on. I want a look at her,' says Pud as he hauls Iska up from the tuft of dunegrass and they shuffle down the path, ducking as they get near the house.

They crouch below the front window, knees in the grit and green-staining weeds. Pud slowly raises his head until his eyes are above the sill and squints against the glass.

'Fat as a cow,' he whispers.

Iska thinks of all those plates of green slime, the earth under her mammy's fingernails.

'She's knitting,' says Pud, 'and not even looking at the needles.'

Iska kneels up and peers into the gloom. It's true, the needles in the changeling mammy's hands are dancing up and down and she is gazing clear out through the opposite window pane towards the sea. The wool that trails over her big moon belly and on to the floor is the fine blue wool her real mammy has been saving, she knows, since Iska was a bab herself. She said it were only for skin that wants softness, and she left it shut up in the sea chest, not even using it when her pa wanted a new vest for the worst of winter.

'What's she making?' Pud asks.

There, below the skipping needles, dangles a small blue sock, so small it might fit on a big toe.

'For her pixie bab, under the marsh where she came from,' breathes Pud, and the glass at his mouth mists up.

Iska picks a spot on the black harbour rocks. She will watch for her pa with his silvery mountain on the blue boat and as soon as she's helped carry in the enormous catch she'll tell it all and Pa will know how to get her real mammy back.

The wind burns her face through the long, white summer days. At home, Skipper stays still as a rug in the hearth, and the sea chest fills up with tiny clothes for the pixie bab. The changeling mammy hardly moves from her grimy bed. The fish stink in the house, already stale, begins to fade.

One afternoon, a shore fisher sidles along the harbour and sits down beside Iska. He tells her his name is Gill Skerry, and he offers her a catfish. The man's face is hidden behind a wad of brown beard, but his voice is kind and he shows Iska how to cook the fish on a stick over a fire he starts up with dry dune-grass. When they scrape the hot flesh from the bones it tastes of smoke.

'Out to see the boats?' he asks.

Iska nods.

'And which one counts for you?'

Iska knows the name because it is the same as her real mammy's name. 'The *Ervet*,' she says.

The shore fisher pauses a moment. 'You sure of that?' His voice has lost its cosiness.

'It's my pa's boat. He named it for Mammy, and he said he'll name the next one for me.' Iska feels sturdier just for saying it.

The shore fisher stays silent a while. He turns a thin spool of line between hands as cragged as the rock they sit on. The wind doesn't seem to touch them. 'I'm sorry, Iska,' he says, in a crackle. 'Your ma all fine up there?' He nods back through the dunes.

Iska feels the cold sluice again through her belly. She can hardly tell about the changeling mammy, silently fattening on soil.

'Might I pay a visit then, Iska? I got more in my basket today than'll do for me and your ma might want to share.'

'No,' she says quickly. 'No, she's sleeping. She'll want leaving alone.'

'Well, you take these two, then.' The shore fisher opens up the basket at his feet and scoops out two silver slithers smeared with red.

Iska forgets her lookout plan, with the fish cold in her palms. One for her, one for Skipper, and the sooner she's home, the sooner she can get the grate warm like her mammy does and have them crisping up.

'And luck to you,' she hears the fisher call as she hurries over the black rocks and into the dunes.

'Skipper!' she shouts on the path, and again at the door. There's not even a whine. 'Skipper!' she tries again when she sees the room empty.

There is a long, high shriek from behind the box bed curtain. As Iska steps forward she feels the slabs slippery under her feet. The thin trail of blue wool from the chair is turned pinky red where it lies across the rug and all around, and daubed on the slabs near the box bed, is more red. Something heaves inside the bed. Something whimpers. She runs then, away from the line of wool, away from the sounds and the certainty of something more dreadful than she's ever thought before.

Her sticky hands are empty by the time she is at the Rincepans' step, and she leaves a red print as she pushes at the door. They are all round the table, Ma and Pa Rincepan and Pud's grown brother Sandy, their brown arms lifting bowls and bread, but it is Pud that Iska looks for.

'She's got Skipper,' she pants, 'she's got him.' But she's lost the rest of the words like she's lost the two fish, somewhere on her way.

'What's this mess?' Ma Rincepan has hold of her wrist in her huge red hand and is poking at her palms. 'Has it come now?'

Iska stares into her frowning face.

'Mercy, what do you do with a girl?' she huffs, and Iska watches her turn and root around in the cupboard, pulling out sheets and flannels. 'Go on then!'

Iska is swept out of the door in the billow of Ma Rincepan's enormous skirt and they are all the way down the hill and along the shore path, sweating and stumbling the pair of them, when she hears another long shriek from her house. She yanks her hand from Ma Rincepan's grip and dodges into the dunes, scrambling against sliding sand, tearing up the whipping fingers of dunegrass. Her pa will help, the boat might be in right now, if she can get to the harbour quick enough, and she skids down the next dune right into the shore fisher's legs.

She feels the rocky hands on her shoulders and sees the wad of brown beard as the fisher crouches to look at her.

'Iska,' says the cosy voice. 'Stop here a moment.'

Her legs wobble as she lets the hands hold her steady. They sit right there in the sand. The breeze still brings howls from the house. Iska wants to tell the shore fisher that it is not her real mammy, that there's a marsh monster in there, but her throat is trapped shut and her lips only shake.

'What a din a fishwife can make, eh?' the man says. 'We'll wait for a bit of peace before we go.'

He is so calm that Iska finds she can breathe it in and her judders calm too. She looks and looks at the lines on the shore fisher's face, the places where there are flecks of white in his beard, the hands still as rocks.

The breeze drops away and so do the sounds from the house. Still they wait.

'Nothing to fear,' the shore fisher says when Iska finally turns to look towards home. A thin whining starts up and she jumps as Skipper leaps in her head. She stays a few steps behind the shore fisher as they make their way up and down the sinking hills of sand, and hangs back at the bean patch while the fisher knocks. Iska hears Granny Turpin's bark, calling them in.

There in the box bed, swathed in Ma Rincepan's sheets, and with Granny Turpin frowning fondly over her, is her mammy. Iska knows it is her because she is humming in that soft song voice, and when she looks up at her, a small smile curls. Iska peers at the bundle in her mammy's lap that is making the whining sounds. It has a small crumpled face like a squashed red flower, its open mouth is the reddest part, and she can see tiny feet like curled red leaves poking out from under the blanket. She thinks of the tiny blue sock. Was it meant for this ugly thing? Where has it come from, and where has the changeling gone? Iska feels the surge of tears again behind her eyes, and looks up at the shore fisher, but this time her real mammy is ready to catch her against her shoulder.

'Thank you, Gill,' her mammy says, and the shore fisher smiles and gives her a bow. 'Now, look, Iska. A brother for you.'

Iska watches her mammy's fingers stroking the wrinkled red face.

'You take proper care of this one,' says Granny Turpin. 'Only one we got.'

Iska stares at her sad face, her mammy's smiling one, and wonders what she can mean.

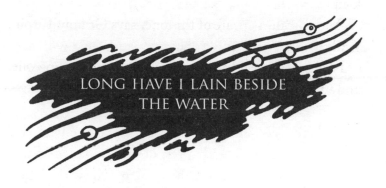

LONG HAVE I LAIN BESIDE THE WATER

GALUSHEN STANDS BEFORE THE mirror and counts. Eighteen years, it has been, since Oline drowned. His love, lost to the river, while her sister Vina watched from the bank. Seventeen years, now, since Galushen and Vina were married. And tomorrow, it will be sixteen years to the day since their daughter May was born. Tomorrow, everything will change.

'Why you bother to keep that mirror, I don't know.' Vina's voice startles him as she sweeps past him in the hallway. She is carrying armfuls of pale green cloth, and when she shakes it out in the light to show him, it shimmers.

'For May?' he asks.

'For my new dress. She'll have quite enough gifts,' Vina says, stroking the fabric, before she rustles away up the stairs.

Galushen has tried to love his wife. He has given her gold and silver, a mountain of finery, rainbows of costly stones. He has filled the house he built for them with mirrors, so that Vina can meet her own admiring gaze whenever she wishes. The mirror he stands before now, in the gloom beneath the staircase, is mottled with age. It is the only furnishing in the house that was not newly made for his wife. Hidden between the backing and the glass is the picture of Oline.

He looks past his reflection, the lined forehead, the black beard flecked with grey, at where he imagines Oline's face looking back at him. Eighteen years. While this house has filled with gifts that have not dampened the echo, that have only cluttered the emptiness; while his daughter has grown and his wife has polished her taste in jewels, Galushen has crept to this mirror to grieve, secretly. The only gifts he brings Oline are stories. If the river had not been running so fast. If she had stepped along the bank more carefully. If Vina had been able to reach her sister's hand. If the sisters had not walked out at all that day. All the stories end the same way, with his wedding to Oline, heart-whole, sure of the world and of his love. Vina's head would soon have been turned by other suitors, and her jealousy forgotten. She was beautiful, after all.

He is about to begin his silent talk with Oline when he hears May's fiddle, the flowing notes of scale after scale, fast and perfect. The sound lifts him. He catches himself smiling in the glass. May, tall and restless, with her tangle of black hair, has become more and more like Oline as she has grown. But this sets her apart, the fierceness she has shown in her fiddle-playing. He listens to her stamp her feet, driving her fingers faster. She finishes the runs of scales with a piercing high note and launches into a wild dance. The music never falters. The playing is flawless. Still, he hears her huff of displeasure when it ends.

In the quiet, he reminds himself of what he came to tell Oline. Tomorrow is his daughter's birthday. May has never been told about her aunt. He agreed to this pact when Vina claimed she would not be able to bear the tactless questions of a child, reminding her of her lost sister at any moment. Galushen has mourned alone, mused alone, and the secret has grown heavier as his daughter has approached the age Oline was when she died. But the agreement ends when May is sixteen, and more than anything, more than the giving of gifts, the merriment, the sight of his daughter's proud face, he is looking forward to the lifting of this burden. If Vina will not share the memory of Oline, he is sure that May will, if only out of curiosity. She will delight in hearing of their likeness. How often he has thought that May could have been Oline's daughter, had she lived.

At the table that evening, Galushen's wife and daughter compose their faces like two beautiful carvings either side of him, and glower at one another. Vina taunts May for her puppy fat. May counts Vina's wrinkles. While they bicker, Galushen eats. He is slow, letting the food melt and meld on his tongue. Tonight it is a pheasant, well-hung. He relishes the dark flesh, the pork fat he has used to roast it. For eighteen years, he has tried to take two mouths' worth of enjoyment from his food. His wife and daughter chew just long enough between speaking to sharpen their barbs.

'You'll grow out of it, as you grew out of dolls, and dressing up in your father's hunting clothes,' says Vina.

'I'll never grow out of it,' May spits. 'I'll die playing the fiddle, if I can. So, I have to go and do this.'

Galushen wipes his mouth. 'Do what?'

'She doesn't play with spirit yet, she says,' Vina starts before May can speak. 'And Quayle the fiddle-master has declared that she must find her spirit. Which sounds like a dreadful game.'

'I can't bear it, how hollow my playing sounds beside his. And it's not a game.'

Vina laughs. 'Hide and seek?'

'I'm not a child,' May shouts, and shoves back her chair.

'You are for one more day,' says Vina.

'Stay,' says Galushen to his daughter, 'she's only teasing.' But May is pulling a long box out from under the table.

She opens it the same way Vina opens her jewel case, ready to feast on treasure. 'It's a mock-up,' she says. She lifts out a fiddle that is pale, rough-skinned, as if left out to weather, but the shape is perfect, each notch and curve. 'All Quayle's apprentices have to make one. It took me a month, at his workshop.' She raises it to her chin, and mimes a bow across the strings. 'Quayle says it's good enough. It proves I'm ready.'

'And what does this mean?' asks Galushen.

'It means I'm to go out and find my fiddle-playing spirit. All the true fiddlers do it. Nine days is long enough, Quayle says. I'll just stay out, and when I find it, I'll make my own fiddle like he did. I'll be able to play like him.'

Vina rolls her eyes. 'But you play perfectly.'

'Yes, I do. Which is why it's time. Quayle says I should go tomorrow.'

'Your birthday?' says Galushen. His daughter's eyes are pleading with him. 'Nine days?'

May nods. 'And then the time to make my fiddle.'

Galushen counts again. How many more days, then, will he have to wait before he can tell her about Oline? His heart will burst. 'I'll speak to Quayle in the morning,' he says.

May crumples in her chair, and Vina smiles, straightening the silver rings on her long fingers.

Galushen rises early, while his daughter sleeps. Vina is already seated before the wide window of their hall, her hands wet with clay. This is Vina's only pastime, when she is not rearranging her rings or her gowns or her tresses. She digs the clay from the riverbank herself – a strange sight, Galushen imagines – and moulds from it small round pots that she seals shut. The house is dotted with them, overgrown seed pods that rattle sometimes, if shaken. Galushen rarely touches them. They irk him, these pots that cannot be used. They smack of contrariness.

'You have her gifts ready?' Vina asks when he stands behind her to look out at the heavy morning sky. The air is damp and chill after weeks of rain, more like the first day of March than the first of May.

'All laid out for her,' he says. He has not told Vina that, as well as hunting garments, he has bought May the finest horse the stables at the High Farm had to offer.

'You've been too generous,' says Vina, and Galushen thinks about the pact, his gift to Vina of sixteen years of silence.

'I have only one daughter,' he replies. He feels Vina bristle. On the day that May was born, he and Vina discovered in the same moment, staring at their daughter's furious red face, that they had both been hoping for a son. Galushen had wanted a hunting companion, an ally in his image. Vina, he supposed, wanted a child who would not trouble her vanity by becoming too beautiful. Or, perhaps, too like Oline. Faced suddenly with this small, screaming girl, Galushen had spoken before he thought, and suggested the name Oline be given in remembrance. Vina had turned her face to the wall. He lost count of how many times he told her, over the days and weeks that followed, that he loved her more than he ever loved Oline. It would not have been enough to say that he loved her differently. Still, Vina did not take to her baby, would not hold her or look at her, as if punishing Galushen for his blunder. He carried his daughter out into the light spring air when she wailed, to spare Vina, and walked with her through the lanes of may blossom. Finally, he had named her for the month of her birth, and learned the first rule for his life as a father: he might love May, but Vina must feel the most loved of all.

'You have only one wife, too,' Vina retorts, dropping her clay, a wet clot, on the table.

Galushen dons his fox-fur hat and walks down the hill towards Neverness village. The sky is sullen, and the ghost of the night's rain prickles his face. He takes a shortcut through the orchard, where the trees drip here and there, and the long grass soaks his boots.

When he reaches the row of workshops at the end of the village, he pauses to listen to the hammering and chinking of the woodcrafters' tools. The first workshop belongs to the women of Neverness. He tried long ago to persuade Vina to join them, to soften the loss of a sister with female company. Wood carvings, the women make; close enough to clay work, Galushen thought, but Vina had refused, preferring solitude.

The door of the last workshop is open. Inside, Quayle the fiddle-master sits with his small feet resting up high on the bench. He is tossing a fiddle bow into the air and catching it by the grip, again and again, and he does not waver as he turns his head and gives a nod of greeting.

'You wish to send my daughter out into the wild, alone,' Galushen says.

Quayle flicks the bow so that it lands to hang neatly on the row of hooks above his head. 'She is ready,' he says. 'You've heard her play. There's nothing left for me to teach her.'

'Then she'll still be ready in a month, a year even.'

Quayle shakes his head. 'Leave it any longer, and life will begin to hurt and harden her. Or else, love might pierce that fresh young heart and ruin it.' He shudders his narrow shoulders in disgust.

'Nine days out there alone will surely be no better for her. Doesn't she play well enough?'

'She plays well enough that, with spirit, she might be a true fiddle-master. She has the desire to do it, and the nimblest fingers. But a fiddler without spirit is like, what?' He glances at Galushen's fur hat, his hunter's coat. 'It's like a fox with no hunger. A stag with no pride.'

'Meaning?'

'Dull. Nobody wants it.'

Galushen pulls off his hat and clenches it behind his back. 'But nine days. Alone, no shelter.'

Quayle leaves his seat and comes to lean by the door. He stands only as high as Galushen's shoulder, yet seems to take up the whole space, blocking the light. 'You can go home and tell her no, and she might as well give up playing today,' he says. 'She could take up clay-work, like her mother. But my hunch is she'll go anyway.'

Galushen thinks of the gifts he has gathered for May, all meant to protect her in the wild, but by his side. He planned to take her hunting, show her the joy of the chase and the kill, but of birds and beasts, not this flimsy idea of spirit. That fine black colt is waiting for her at the High Farm stables even now. After he'd watched Madden, the stable hand there, ride the animal for him, he'd been seized by how much stronger, how much safer, a girl looked on horseback. He'd had a job of coaxing Trick and Robin to sell it, and had made a rash offer in the end, to secure that same strength for his daughter. He wants her to take it. 'If she's to go out on a hunt, then, might she ride?' he asks.

Quayle gives a high laugh.

'Then how does a man – or indeed a girl – hunt down this spirit, as you call it?'

Quayle leaves the door and goes to the corner of the workshop, where a fiddle leans in the shadow. 'I'd been out six days. Hadn't eaten; nothing but stream water and bits of herbs I found. I was at the shore, cold, wretched, the dark coming down, and when I got to the far end, I heard it.' He picks up the fiddle and walks towards Galushen with it tucked under his chin. 'The roar in the cave there; it sang chords to me.' He begins to draw his bow across the strings.

More notes than Galushen can count are tumbling from the fiddle, clashing in his heart. The tune rolls low and tugs deep in his chest, the moon tugging a tide.

'Spent the whole night in the cave.' Quayle's voice is raised over the storm of music that seems too strong, too sad, to be breaking from one small man. As it goes on, it conjures images in mist, a boat lost in the endless black, a voice deep in a cave. Galushen is enraged and enchanted at once, for while the sadness of the song makes him want to think of lost love, of Oline, he cannot summon her to mind. The music tells of someone else's loss.

When Quayle stops playing, it is like the sigh of a wave sinking back beneath itself. 'See?' he says.

Galushen takes the fiddle and notes that the pegs that hold the strings taut are smoothed dripstones, snapped from a cave roof. The neck is driftwood, the fingerboard a mosaic of flat scallop shells. He admires the fine work of piecing them together into a thing of such beauty, both in sight and sound. He holds it to his ear and hears the faint hiss of the sea.

'You made this afterwards?'

'May will do the same.'

'And the song that you played?'

'It entered the fiddle, as it entered me, too,' Quayle says. 'It belongs to the cave. A memory left there.'

Galushen walks home the longer way, where the path is not so steep. It passes the river, so high after the April rain that it is washing away the bank, sending clumps of grass into the swirling current. The water is deep brown. He can hear May practising as he climbs the hill, nearing the house. It's a jig he knows, ladders and whirligigs of notes that run away with themselves, and that he has felt proud to hear her play. But now he can feel the lack in it, beside Quayle's conjuring. The pang the fiddle-master left in his chest has not fully faded.

May is playing in front of the largest mirror in the house. She has found the pile of gifts Galushen left for her, and put them all on. The garments were meant only to shield his daughter from the wind and wet; he did not think how she would look, wearing them. Now, in the russet deerskin cape, the black leather gaiters, the red fox-fur cap atop her hank of black hair, she looks like a blood-stained huntress.

'Thank you,' she calls as he passes behind her, and she plays harder, louder, smacking her bow down against the strings.

There is lustiness in her playing at least. Quayle's song was mournful, a feeling familiar to Galushen but one he does not want his daughter to know too well. If she learns to play with spirit, does that mean pain, too? May is so young. She is a joy to him. He wants that joy to remain, for it to suffuse them both when he tells her about Oline.

At the table, Vina smiles at May as if a harsh word had never passed between them. 'Nine days without an hour of fiddle practice,' she says. 'That must be the best of your birthday gifts.'

'Much longer,' says May. She has kept on the cape. 'After I've found my spirit, I have to make my new fiddle. I can't play the plain one then, can I?'

Galushen chews but can hardly taste the deer meat. He is counting again, the number of days this might take, until he can share the truth with his daughter.

'And where might you look, on your great hunt?' Vina is still smiling. She has dressed today in a pale cloud-grey, with silver glinting at her throat and wrists, so close to the silver of her hair that Galushen keeps glancing at it. Her hair had changed while she was carrying May, the redhead he had married fading to a silver-headed mother. The shock of losing a sister, he'd supposed, finally showing itself in her body when it did not show in her demeanour.

'I won't just be looking,' May replies. 'It's not like a game of hide and seek.'

'How will you know when you've found it?' Galushen asks.

May is looking hard at her mother, trying to wither the smile still fixed on her lips. 'It will be a new feeling. Not like any other. I'll know.'

Galushen gives up on his meat. His mouth is dry, and he takes a great gulp of wine. Vina does not look at him, but goes on questioning and encouraging May. She sounds delighted with the whole plan. When May takes her advice and goes to begin packing the food and belongings she will need, Galushen waits until she is out of earshot, and takes another long draught from his cup.

'Today should have been the day to tell her,' he says.

Vina's smile is sly. 'That you've spent half your fortune on a horse for a gift, and she can't even take it with her? Trick and Robin will be laughing at you in the ale room for months, getting drunk on your gold.'

'No, not that.' Galushen's cheeks are burning.

'Then what?'

'The pact. Sixteen years, we agreed. Then she would be old enough, and time would have passed to ease your memory.'

Vina is staring at him. 'You cannot be thinking of that.' Her eyes are cold, testing.

'What else? I kept my promise, I've said nothing. There's no need to keep such a secret any longer.'

'All these years, and you are still thinking of her?' Vina hisses, as May runs past the open door and up the stairs. 'How dare you?' Her chair screeches and clatters to the stone floor as she stands, still holding her cup of wine.

'But we must tell her.'

'Oh, spare me.' Her voice is a growl. Wine flies from her cup as she throws up her arms. 'You think she doesn't know? That she has never heard so much as a whisper all this time? The village is full of gossip. She has friends – that urchin-child Gad, for one, always prattling. You're a fool if you think there's any secret to be told.'

Galushen reaches out a hand to calm her, but she jerks away and lets the cup fall and shatter on the stone.

'You married me, Galushen. It's me who's been here with you, sixteen years and longer,' she shouts. 'It's me you love.'

Galushen watches his wife storm from the room, her bracelets clashing. He drains the wine from the jug and swallows it down to quell the burn of shame in his throat. If it's true, that May knows all about Oline, that she no more wants to talk of her than Vina does, he is indeed a fool. And worse, one whose daughter has never asked him, has never come to hear the truth from his mouth.

The three of them stand together by the stump of the oak tree that used to shade the back of the house. Galushen misses that tree, lost in the Great Storm. But he will miss his daughter more. May is wearing the russet cape, the red fox-fur cap, and has on her shoulder the bag Galushen made, with knife, flask, flint and cured meat all inside. Vina pats her daughter's shoulder and smiles her farewells, but Galushen seizes her and will not loose her from his arms.

'If you pass by here, leave me a sign,' he whispers through her hair. 'Don't be afraid to give up.'

May nods. She pulls away from him, and as she runs down the hill she waves her arms in goodbye, but does not turn. He watches her cape flying in the squally air, until she is as small as a blood-red bead rolling into the trees at the valley bottom.

When she has been gone only a few hours he goes to the oak stump, looking for some mark she might have left. He kicks at the few heads of clover that are poking from the grass, then sits there until the last smudge of light has left the sky.

The next morning, he wakes with a start, and remembers. He should not have let May go. He should not have listened to Vina, either. His mind's eye roves the most treacherous places his daughter could be wandering: the deep clefts along the coast; the shore cave; the steep-sided headland. It is still dark, but dawn is a fine time for a huntsman to be out, should anyone see him. He searches for his slingshot and tramps down the hill towards the wood.

The rain has stopped, but the world is deep in dew. His daughter has slept out, somewhere, in this dank, chilled place. There are wood pigeons, dozy on their roosts. There will be grouse, a few pheasants, nestled in the low bushes. He walks in the half-hearted light of dawn, the slingshot dangling loose at his side. The wider paths have been trodden recently. Someone has hacked a few wands from a hazel tree. When he reaches the edge of the wood he can hear the river, rushing, swollen, eating away at its banks. He wonders where Vina comes to dig the clay for her maddening pots.

Hunger begins to nag his stomach, along with doubt. May is bold, and he has taught her to look after herself out here. She wouldn't risk the clefts, or the cave. And if Vina was right, and May already knows about Oline, it can wait a little longer before he speaks to her. He can find a way of broaching it that will not reveal his foolishness. What he cannot shake off is the anger, that he could have confided in her long ago, and been rid of this burden of secrecy.

Vina looks up from her clay when Galushen throws his hat down on to the window seat and slumps beside it. 'No kills?' she says, eyeing the slingshot. 'Nobody has ever died from spending a few days out in the woods, you know. Your daughter is tough.' She digs her thumbs hard into a hump of clay and splits it.

Has nobody ever died, sent by Quayle to find their spirit? It's a fine day, but the weather could change any hour of day or night. He remembers the Great Storm, Pike Lightfoot washed to his death in the shore cave, and that daughter of his, the same age May is now, out in the wind and rain. He shudders, and gazing out through the window, he asks the sky to stay bright. Then he pulls his knife from his pocket and digs a notch in the edge of the window seat to mark the passing of one night. Eight more, and she will be home.

Vina wipes the grey slick from her fingers and comes to lean at his shoulder. 'You've brought the forest back with you. I can smell beasts.' She lets her hair rain down on his face as she sniffs at his neck. 'We're alone.'

Galushen hears the silence in the house, louder in his ears than the dance of May's fiddle every morning.

'Isn't it pleasant?' Vina says. 'Nobody here but us.' She bends to kiss him but he turns away, and looks out through the glass.

'She could be anywhere out there,' he says. He gets up, leaving her in the window seat, and hears her knock his slingshot to the floor as he retreats from the room.

On the second day, the morning is sweet with sunshine. Galushen finds Vina sitting on a chair by the oak stump. Freckled by sunlight through the shade, his wife looks like a silver nymph.

'That's May's chair,' he says. It is the one he had carved to match their own at the table, when his daughter was grown enough to sit with them.

'But she's not here. And this is my house. Ours,' she adds. 'Bring your own. Join me.'

'Aren't you worried for her?'

Vina stretches out her arms, and beckons him, the rings on her fingers gleaming. 'She'll be loping around at Quayle's workshop, or sneaking to see her friends. Why don't you just enjoy this? I'm all yours. You're all mine.'

He does not believe this. He does not want to believe anything Vina has said to him the last few days.

'You're lying,' he says. 'And I want to tell my daughter the truth, tell her about Oline.'

'Why do you still harp on?' Vina's smile has become a snarl. 'Your life is full, and rich, and sweet, and you want to sour it. You're even more of a fool than I thought.'

Galushen turns his back on her and looks, again, to be sure that May has left no sign for him on the stump, before retreating to the house.

Later, when Vina goes to the village, he picks up one of her sealed pots from the mantelpiece and blows the dust from it. When he shakes it, he hears something slide inside. He squeezes, but the round form resists, so he cracks it against the wall and splits it open. A bead falls into his palm, red glass. It nudges a memory but he cannot grasp it before it sinks again into the dark.

How will May really know when her hunt is over, he wonders. If she must feel something wholly new, he wants it to be a joyful feeling. Not like the exquisite ache he heard in Quayle's playing, so like the ache that began in him when Oline died. He finds himself standing in front of the mottled mirror, rolling the red glass bead between his fingers. The ache has muted a little, perhaps, in the passing years, but never gone. *Is it because we never said our farewells?* he asks Oline's picture behind the glass. Even when Vina wept and told the story, how her sister had slipped, how she herself had been rooted there on the bank, frozen, while Oline was swept downstream; even when she said that by the time she shook sense back into her limbs, stripped off her skirt and tried to step into the cold water, it was too late; the knowledge of how it ended did not help him. And nobody had ever found Oline, who would have floated white as a swan in that brutish water.

On the third day, Quayle comes to the house. When Galushen opens the door, fear tolls in his heart.

'No news,' Quayle laughs. 'I was wandering nearby, and thought I might come and play the minstrel.'

Galushen wants to shut the door in his face, but Vina comes flitting, bright and alert as a bird, blushing as Quayle kisses her hand. She laughs when he jokes that May must be jealous, to have such a beautiful mother.

When Quayle gets out his fiddle, Galushen leaves and goes back to the oak stump. He does not know what his daughter would choose to leave as a sign for him. A feather, perhaps, which has blown away.

Music bleeds from the house. He tries not to listen, but the sound is bewitching, a song that seems to come from under the sea. It is the same song Quayle played at the workshop. He creeps back towards the house, drawn by the strange sorrow, the longing that matches his own, but refuses to let it take full shape in his heart. Quayle draws the song to an end when he enters the room.

Vina is still as a stone on the window seat. 'Will you play another, a different tune?' she asks.

'Whatever I play, the song, the essence of it, will be the same,' Quayle says.

'Why is that?' asks Galushen.

'The fiddle took something from the sea cave, when I made it from the pieces I found there. It tells that tale.'

'And do you know what it means?'

Quayle gives him a quizzical look. 'You've only to listen,' he says. And while he plays again, Galushen sees the girl weeping in the cave, the father lost to the waves. He understands the loss that is not his own.

'What a tall tale,' Vina smirks, when Quayle has gone. 'I suppose he thinks it's romantic.'

'Didn't you hear it?' Galushen says.

'It's just music. Just clever music,' says Vina, and she hums the song, again and again through the afternoon, turning it into an empty tune that grates at Galushen's ears.

That evening, May's chair is not back at the table. He eats hastily, thinking about the dried meat he put in May's bag, whether it was enough. He refuses to stroll with Vina at dusk. When she has slammed the door and stalked away, he goes to cut the third notch into the window seat, then marks where he will put the next.

On the fourth day, the red glass bead is gone from his pocket. Galushen skulks through the house, shaking each of Vina's pots, gathering those that rattle. He cracks them one by one, emptying out more red beads, an ochre one, and two a kind of silvery blue. He arranges them along the line in his palm. The memory does not fall back into the dark this time. He sees Oline's black hair tangled with her necklace of these beads, one day when they lay together on the headland, breathing the rich scent of the flowering gorse.

What does she mean by this? he asks the mirror. *If she has kept a necklace of yours, why does she hide it, when I would love to share in this remembrance?* His face is twisting in

146

the glass. He is ashamed to see himself weep. Was Vina as jealous of these beads as she was jealous of her sister, of his love for Oline? He has given Vina a mine's worth of precious stones, far more beautiful, more valuable, than a few glass beads. It is a strange kind of remembrance, to seal them away, but perhaps that's all it is. Perhaps by doing this, Vina has done what he has not, and found a place to lay her grief, and let go. If he cannot yet undo the secret and speak to May, he can at least do this. He will let Oline go too, and live with memory, not grief. His heart might then love wholly again.

His feet pounding with purpose, Galushen marches down the hill, into the wood. He cuts a straight path through, and squints at the sun as he steps out from between the trees on the other side and starts along the riverbank. The water glints in the clear, strong light. It is still running fast, even though the weeks of rain are over. He squeezes the handful of beads in his pocket. Somewhere here, Oline slipped. Somewhere, she struggled and was swept down. He follows the river further, towards the bend where a willow tree stands. The kind of place two sisters might linger. The roots of the tree are like twisting steps down the bank. He flinches to think of Oline's feet on slippery bark, and goes on, following the current down, past the bend.

There on the rippling, ridging surface of the water he sees a dark mass, long black hair flowing. As he stares, it vanishes, and he looks up, to be sure it was not a bird shadow. After a few moments he sees it again, further downstream. He stumbles along the bank, his eyes on the rag of black, and is certain he sees a head rise from the water, as if to breathe, before diving down again. 'Oline,' he calls, as it vanishes, but the rough thrum of his own voice makes him stop in shame. He must look like a man losing his mind. As he watches, the head rises again, and turns. He sees the pale face beneath the black hair. So like Oline, his daughter. She is swimming back, strong against the current.

Galushen dodges behind a tree, not daring to look lest she see him. He remembers Vina standing waist high in the gentle pool not far from here, teaching the young May to swim, holding her in the water, coaxing, fierce when May whined at the cold. No wonder she wanted her daughter to know how to float, how to hold herself up against a flow. He peers around the tree and sees the pile of May's belongings on the far bank, the russet cape, the fox-fur hat. When she has swum past he lets himself watch her for a little while. He should stay and make sure she is safe, in this flooded, swollen river. When she is far enough away upstream, he goes to watch the black smudge of her head, bobbing, dipping. He takes the glass beads from his pocket and holds them, ready to drop into the water, then puts them back.

When he reaches home, Vina is pacing by the oak stump. The shards of the pots he smashed are gathered in a pile amongst the roots. She has not seen him, and he waits for her to turn. When she does, she gives a little yelp.

He kneels in the grass among the clover flowers and pot fragments, and reaches out his hands. 'Forgive me,' he says, 'for breaking them.' He hangs his head and waits for her to come to him. When she does not, he looks up and sees that she has covered her face. Her shoulders are shaking. 'But I'm glad, Vina, to know that you have not really forgotten. That you miss her as I do.'

She peers at him between her fingers. Her breathing slows. He goes to embrace her, his beautiful wife, and she falls against his chest, silent.

That night, while his wife is sleeping, he takes a candle to the mottled mirror. His face in the glass is tired, but peaceful. Vina had been so happy, and so hungry, when he let her lead him to their bed, that he had not fully undressed before she was sliding against him, pulling his heat against her coolness, whispering his name until it sounded like rushing water. Still, he woke afterwards from a dream of Oline. He wants to love his wife.

He sets down the light and lifts the mirror from the wall. The nails in the frame come loose with no more than a tug, and he prises up the backing. The picture of Oline falls in fragments to the floor. He tries to piece them together but the image has mouldered. There is no longer any face or imprint of black hair. When he hangs the mirror back on the wall and holds the candle up, there is a shadow now, where patches of silvering have come away from the glass. Perhaps he will get rid of it, and put a picture of his wife and daughter in its place.

On the ninth day, Galushen wakes entwined with Vina. He creeps from the bedroom and makes his way down to the village in warm sunshine. By the path and field edges, may blossom is turning the hedgerows to white froth. In the village, the door of the workshop is open and there, at the workbench, is May. She is sliding a plane, and he listens to the soft rasps, sighs from the wood.

'At work already?'

May turns. Her face is shadowy, her lips pale, but she smiles. 'I've been here five days. I found what I needed, and I wanted to begin on the fiddle right away. Quayle gave me a bed in the loft, and I've worked, all night sometimes.'

He goes to join her at the workbench but she holds up a palm.

'Let me finish it before you see. Quayle says I'll be done in less than a week if I keep on like this.' Even though she is tired, there is a dark light in her eyes.

'But you're well?'

She nods, and turns to the bench, sweeping a blizzard of wood shavings to the floor. 'I'll come home as soon as it's ready,' she calls, picking up the plane.

Galushen thinks of little except how best to welcome his daughter home. He is careful not to let Vina see how much it fills his head. She has been so contented, so loving, the last few days like a honeymoon delayed. He chooses the best of their meat and wine for a feast. He roams the hillsides, as far as Murnon's sheep fields, where the hedgerows are high. When he is sure nobody sees him, he cuts branches of may blossom to fill his hunting sack.

When the day comes, he stands at the window with a view of the path up from the village, and waits. Clouds roll across the sky and by the time the rusty red and black figure appears it is raining, grey sheets that billow over the slope. May climbs the hill slowly. He roots himself to keep from running down to meet her and to take the box she is carrying, held tenderly against her chest.

Finally, his daughter is home, standing in a room filled with white sprays. Her cape drips on to the floor, which is already dotted with fallen blossom. He embraces her, the box still in her arms, and feels her tremble. She is wan, her face dark and her lank hair tangled, and Vina stares when she comes to greet her daughter.

'Drink some wine,' Galushen offers her a cup from the table, but she shakes her head.

'Let me play first,' she says, looking at Vina all the while.

'If you want, but then you must eat.' His daughter's solemn eyes pain him.

May goes to the far end of the long room while Galushen sits, Vina beside him, at the table. She lays down the russet cape and sodden fur cap and, with her back turned, opens the case. She lifts the fiddle to her chin and raises her bow. Galushen grasps his wife's hand. Still facing away, May begins, drawing the bow slow and hard across the strings.

Galushen closes his eyes as sound fills the room. It is rich as raven black, as glowing black hair, but with a ghostly light, high notes like glimpses of white. He feels cold. As the music grows it begins to writhe, and as May's fingers bend and press at the strings, he sees pale hands reaching. The raven black is not feathers, or hair. It is the weight of water, the shock of icy cold in his chest. The notes turn, fast and frantic. Struggle pulses through him. He cannot open his eyes but only feels himself flailing against the hands that catch about his head and push him down. The music is so loud he cannot breathe. The hands grip and push, and he cannot raise his head against their force. He sways in the cruel melody. He is weak in its current, even as it grows muffled and begins to fade. Then he breathes in the last soaring note until it wavers to a hiss, and there is silence.

After some moments, he senses Vina, rigid in her chair. Her fingernails have dug into his palm and he looks at the four red crescents there, in the crease.

'Bring it here,' he says.

'No,' Vina shouts, and she is running from the table, to the far end of the room, where she tries to snatch the fiddle from her daughter's grasp. May holds it high, out of reach, and twists away from her mother.

She comes and lays the fiddle on the table before Galushen. The neck is white, a long, polished bone. The pegs that wind the strings are the same: thin, white spindles. He turns the fiddle over in his hands. Embedded in the smooth back of the body is a red glass bead. He places his finger on it, cool in the warm wood.

'Did you give her this bead?' he calls to Vina. She does not answer, only stands and stares with wild eyes. 'Then where did it come from?'

'The river,' says May, 'where I found my spirit. I swam there, and it was the sound of the water in my ears, how it swept around me and into me like music. I swam until I was very cold, right down where it gets near the sea. I dived under, to listen to the water, and I found these things to make the fiddle.'

'The bead?'

'Yes.'

'And this?' Galushen points to the neck, the white pegs.

'All bone. Buried in the bank.'

Vina's hands are gripped in her silver hair. He sees the same hands that pushed through the black of May's music, the hands that drowned a sister, who pleaded, but could not fight.

'What's the matter?' May asks.

Galushen looks at his daughter, the image of Oline, and then at his wife. Their faces are like two beautiful carvings, one sad, one stricken, as they gaze back at him.

There are no mirrors in Galushen's house. When he sits at his table, his daughter on his left side, he tries to enjoy the meat he eats, but tastes only earth. His wine is like brown river water in his mouth. Each meal is a penance.

He asks May to play for him sometimes. She will be fiddle-master after Quayle, the best player that Neverness has. They like to walk together, along the river, and watch the water swirling against the muddy banks. They sit by the willow tree, and Galushen tells his daughter about his first love. May imagines what love will be like, the warmth that will soften the chill in her heart. She lets her father talk as long as he wants. He has endured so many years of silence. When he has finished, she takes her fiddle and stands beneath the willow's waving fronds. While she plays, her fingers pressing into the long neck of bone, Galushen closes his eyes and listens to his lost love, calling from the water, calling through the dark.

VERLYN'S BLESSINGS

VERLYN WEBBE HAS A wing in place of an arm. It is too large, the grey speckled feathers reaching down to his ankle. The weight of it has pulled his shoulders out of kilter. He wears a coat to hide the crookedness in his body that is otherwise strong, the wing filling out one sleeve like a burst bolster with feathers poking from the cuff.

Every morning, when he goes to the lean-to behind his house to work, Verlyn counts his blessings. The first is his wife, Werrity. 'I am lucky to have her,' he reminds himself, as he sweeps the floor, turning the broom in his one, strong hand. He does not use his wing to sweep, though Werrity once said it might be made useful for something, at least, if he did. 'I was lucky to find her, and to keep her.' Werrity, the only woman on the island who would marry a man with a wing in place of an arm. She chose him in spite of it. She had her reasons. He does not mind that she makes him sleep with the wing on the outside of the bed, lest it brush against her in the night.

When the sweeping is done, Verlyn picks up a half-made creel and begins to work. Despite the wing, he is a skilful weaver of baskets, and wattle for fences. This basket is for his brothers, the next blessing that he counts. He is thankful for all six of them, for their hearts big enough to dive long and deep, and to share with their seventh brother the best of their haul brought up from the bottom of the sea.

His one strong hand works fast in the lean-to. He built it there behind the house a few years ago when, for Werrity's sake, he stopped working in the yard out front in view of passing villagers. He has ways of holding the willow fronds tight in his teeth and between his knees, so his fingers can make the weave. Werrity was pleased with this skill when she married him. It took years for her to grumble at the pace of his work, and point out what two hands might do with the same nimble tricks.

As he bends and tucks the last willow fronds of the new creel, Verlyn's final blessing, his son, Marram, comes running from the house. Despite Werrity's fears, Marram was born with just a tuft of down poking from under one thumbnail. The first thing Werrity did with the new babe in her arms was to take his tiny thumb in her mouth and bite the feathers away.

Now that Marram is seven years old and strong enough to squirm from his mother's grasp, he refuses the scissors wielded at his thumb. It has always been

Werrity who has snipped at him, a wing being as useless for holding a wriggling child as it is for holding a baby. It was many months after the birth that his wife first let Verlyn cradle his son against his chest. She bent close, in case Marram should writhe from his one strong hand. He forgave her this easily, for she'd once lost a bab, when young. He forgave that she would not let him support that warm little body with his wing.

Marram is hiding his thumb in his mouth, safe from scissors. Verlyn pulls it out again.

'Little man, that's for babs,' he says. He lifts the creel. 'Let's take this to the shore. Your uncles' boat will be coming in.'

He leads Marram out along the shore path, where damselflies drowse in the warmth. The sea glints under hazy sun. Seagulls are wheeling and crying, waiting for a catch. Down on the beach, wind buffets the marsh grass in the dunes and tweaks at the tip of Verlyn's wing, sending ripples of ache through his shoulder and into his bent back.

They walk until they reach the largest fishing hut. Across the front, high white letters spell out the name WEBBE. The sea is ruffled green and white beyond, with no sign of the Webbe boat.

Marram runs away along the foamline, chasing the sea in and out. Verlyn nudges the hut door and pushes the creel into the gloom. When he turns the corner to the sunny side of the hut, the light flooding his vision, there, sitting against the wall, is a woman. He shades his eyes and sees that it is Linnet Lundren.

Linnet Lundren eats oysters raw. The youngest of Verlyn's six brothers, Drake, told him this, laughing. None of the Webbes will eat the oysters and scallops they pull up from the sea bed until they have been crisped up hot with mutton fat. All spring, Linnet has been coming to wait like a cat by the Webbe hut, and when Drake passes her a handful fresh off the boat, she shucks them right there on the stones. Drake is the only Webbe brother not yet married, though he is the handsomest. Verlyn has seen the way Linnet's looks slide over his brother's sleek limbs when he leaps from the sea.

Linnet has her eyes closed, her round face turned up towards the sun. Verlyn is about to retreat but she opens one eye and smiles.

'Here,' she says, 'if you're waiting for those mer-men brothers of yours.' She picks a small, pale green apple from the pile nestled in her lap and holds it out.

'Apples won't be ripe for months,' Verlyn says. 'Why eat them sour?'

Linnet picks out another and bites hard, wincing as she chews. She is looking at him, sucking at the bitter juice. 'Why d'you keep it tucked away?' she asks. Verlyn glances down at the grey feathers poking from his sleeve. 'You didn't always. I remember.'

As a boy, Verlyn did not cover his wing. The villagers were used to him and mostly paid no heed – except for the other children. He went along with the games in the schoolyard. Whether he played the angry dragon or the timid swan, it always ended in a crowd of children, including Werrity, squealing and scattering away from the touch of feathers. One day, a girl stayed behind when the others fled. She stood beside him, solemn, and asked to touch the wing. She ran her fingers across the long quills as across harp strings, and the sweet twinge in his shoulder bone surprised him.

'Now me,' the girl said. She stood with her eyes screwed shut and her hands tight by her sides. Verlyn swept the wing over her head, letting the feathers drift over her shoulders. She stayed very still for a long time, her chest rising and falling, and then ran away to follow the others. Afterwards, he wondered how he'd known that was what she wanted.

Linnet Lundren is not so different now she is grown, her corn-yellow plait of hair unravelling around her curious face, and stolen apples in her plump hands.

'They'll be in soon,' he says, turning to look out at the sea. The boat has rounded the outcrop of rock, and they watch the six seal-headed Webbe brothers pulling their oars with twelve burnished arms. They leap into the shallows and tug the boat on to the shingle. One lifts Marram on to his high shoulders and the others swing baskets up from the boat to carry them. They gleam with pride, shaking salt from their hair.

When they reach the hut they slap Verlyn's back in greeting with warm, sea-salty hands. He never shows that this hurts. His brothers grin, but are sheepish. The baskets they lay down by the hut have only a few shells in the bottom, resting in nests of kelp.

'Sorry, Linnet. None spare,' says Drake. He winks at Verlyn.

Linnet holds out handfuls of apples to him. 'I've these for you, though,' she smiles.

'Look worse than raw oysters,' Drake laughs. 'They're not ripe.' He wanders off to rub away the last of the salt from his skin, and spread himself in the sun with the others. Lying on the stones, they take turns to lift Marram up on their feet, where he stretches out his arms to dive.

Verlyn takes one of Linnet's apples. She sidles up close to him so the warmth of her round hip presses against his. She is still looking at Drake, but she whispers in Verlyn's ear, 'I've not forgotten. I wish you'd do it once more.'

Verlyn's brothers have told him before of Linnet Lundren's wanton whispers in the village ale room, but still her voice sends a shiver down his neck. She bends and runs her hand over the long quill tips that jut from his coat sleeve. Verlyn drops the apple from his hand.

At home, while Werrity scrapes scallops from their shells and scolds Marram for trailing sand across the floor, Verlyn takes a pail of water out to his lean-to. He does not mind that he is forbidden from washing his wing in the house. It is true that wet feathers smell musty and stick to the floor. He shakes off his coat and holds the wing out with effort. When he flexes, it aches. He so rarely moves it, now that he keeps it hidden. Whatever tendons used to let him raise it to feel the wind's lift have shrunk and stiffened. It is a sad sight, the feathers matted with being pressed inside his sleeve.

While he douses it, parting the quills at the roots with his fingers to wet in between, he recalls again the moment years ago, in the schoolyard, when he touched Linnet Lundren's head with his feather tips. How much stronger the wing felt then, even though his body was already bent. He hears the grown Linnet's words in his ear, and wonders at her boldness.

He sits outside to let the breeze dry him, wing spread as best he can, and catches Werrity frowning from the casement. A moment later she comes running out, and shoos him into his lean-to.

'Don't let Marram see,' she hisses. 'I try all day to get him to snip that thumbnail.' She won't call it a feather. 'Must you sit out brazen like that?' She stands in the doorway and turns to look out towards the sea.

The wing is heavy with water still. Verlyn rests it awkwardly across his workbench.

'I don't want Marram thinking he'll turn out the same,' says Werrity.

Verlyn wonders if he was meant to hear.

'I want him to grow up strong like his uncles,' she says and bustles back to the house, without looking at his wing, without looking at him.

Next day, Verlyn is carrying new wattle panels up to the High Farm for Trick and Robin, Werrity's rough-skinned uncles, when he pauses on the lane. The wind has dropped and the sun beats down. He is sweating under his coat. The lane runs alongside the orchard, where shade pools green beneath the trees. One of the trees is shaking its branches. He pushes the orchard gate, and sees a round white arm reaching for unripe fruit, and a skirt lifted high to catch them. It is Linnet Lundren.

'Not at the shore?' Verlyn asks.

'Your brother doesn't want my gifts,' she says. She lets the apples roll into the grass and walks towards him. 'Why d'you always wear that coat?' She smiles, and tugs at the sleeve that is tight with the wing inside. Her wily face comes close to his. Her skin smells of sun. 'I've not forgotten. I wish you'd do it again.'

Verlyn lets her pull the coat off him, and she hangs it on a low branch. The wing, newly washed, springs wide from his shirt where it is torn off at the shoulder. It is like unlacing a tight boot. The cool of the orchard shade washes through it.

Linnet circles him, her gaze fixed on the long, grey feathers. 'Will you?' she asks, and bows her head. He raises the wing and sweeps it over her, letting the feathers brush her shoulders, her neck, her hair, letting them drift over her face. It hurts his back, but above the pain there is a sweet note that sings through the quills where they touch Linnet, and flows through his shoulder blade, up the back of his neck. When he stops, she is still for a long time. Then she opens her eyes just long enough to say, 'Again.'

This is how it begins. In the days, then weeks, that follow, Verlyn sets out from his lean-to with pieces of his work, or he pretends to, or he just goes walking. The village sleeps, hot in summer's open mouth. In the orchard, in the perfumed maze of the headland gorse, or by the bank of the stream that lazes muddily now down the hill, he meets Linnet Lundren.

She brings him gifts. Sour apples, but also warm hen's eggs, smooth white pebbles, a honeysuckle flower, a pair of wood pigeons. Whatever these things mean, whether he wants them or not, he always gives what she wants in return.

Through the summer, Linnet's white roundness turns golden, her forehead and neck freckling. Verlyn's wing grows stronger. He can open it wide now, feel the breeze take it. He washes it, fluffs out the down between the long feathers, thinking of Linnet and the way the sly wildness goes out of her when he strokes her head. The twinges of pleasure when he does this, spreading from the feathers into his shoulder and across his scalp, flow deeper and last longer. He lets them seize him. While Linnet's eyes are closed, he looks at her neck, her soft arms, her fingers pressing together where she holds her hands at her sides. He feels a yearning for life that he has not felt since youth.

Every morning, when he brushes out the lean-to, Verlyn counts his blessings. His six big-hearted brothers, who share their harvest dived from the land under the sea. Marram, learning to swim now, in the calmer summer waters. Werrity, who married him in spite of his wing.

He remembers how, when he wooed Werrity, they met in places hidden from village eyes: the tumbledown cottage at the wood's edge, the sheltered wall nooks of Murnon's sheep fields, the curtained shade of the river's willow trees. Now Verlyn pictures himself in these spots with Linnet Lundren. As his courtship of Werrity grew more deliberate, he tried once to caress her neck with his feathers. He knew she'd been free with her favours before, and had wanted his turn. She squealed and shook him away, and the look in her eye told him not to do it again. Since then it has only been his own hand that has touched the wing, and then only to wash it, digging his fingers deep where the feather shafts push from the bone.

Can he count Linnet Lundren as one of his blessings now? It is because of Linnet that he holds himself straighter, braving the pain in his spine. Because of her his wing has grown strong, and he likes to look at it again, feeling the sinews stretch when he spreads it wide. He feels some of the pride he sees in his brothers, when they stride back to their hut laden with treasure. The coat, and his shirts with one sleeve torn away, lie in a heap under his workbench. Whenever he can, he wears only weather on his skin, on his feathers.

The summer turns silver. Every moth that stirs the evening air sets Verlyn's skin alight. The warm breeze through the marsh grass, its hush and scent of sun, makes him quiver. He meets Linnet Lundren more often in the wood, where they stand in the shade and say less and less to one another before she bows her head for feathers. In all their meetings, he has not touched her with his one, strong hand. It is only ever wing on skin, and the more Verlyn's wing tells him Linnet's skin is smoother than the pebbles she brings, smoother than milk, the more he wishes to feel with his fingertips.

One hazy morning, the air thick with heat, he comes into the house bare-chested to find Werrity chasing Marram once again with the scissors. Verlyn snatches them and stands between his wife and his son. Marram clings to his side and he encloses him beneath his wing.

'It's one feather,' Verlyn says. 'Leave him be.'

Werrity claws at him for the scissors, scratching his hand. 'Cover yourself up,' she shouts. 'Have you no shame?'

He pulls Marram closer under his wing, against his skin.

'What's got into your head, Verlyn Webbe?' Werrity shouts.

'Perhaps it's pride,' he says.

Werrity's eyes narrow. 'Who's told you to show yourself off? Is that how you're going about all those hours when you should be at your work?'

'I'll do as I please.'

Afterwards, in the lean-to, he fidgets with the willow fronds that slide across his sweating fingers. It is too close to breathe. He wishes Marram had a whole wing instead of only one feather, so that he might one day sweep it over a woman in the quiet cool of the wood. He wishes Werrity could see him with Linnet Lundren. He kicks away the struts he had clasped between his knees and walks down the side of the house, through the patch of withering nettles, towards the shore.

There is no sign of Linnet at the Webbe hut. He waits a while, his wing stretched to feel the breeze, listening to the waves rake the shingle and the seagulls crying. These sounds become the crackle of Linnet's footsteps, the curl of her voice in his ear.

He hears the Webbe boat being dragged up the beach, and watches his brothers grin and jostle as they walk along the stones. As they come to flop down around Verlyn in a glistening heap, he sees there are only five of them.

'Where's Drake?' he asks.

They shrug their broad shoulders and shake water from their dark heads. He can feel the life beating in their unbent bodies, the thrum of those gigantic hearts. It is the same thrum that rises in him when his wing passes over Linnet Lundren's skin.

Verlyn leaves the five Webbes dozing in the sun and hunts, shirtless, through the outskirts of the village. All the places he has been with Linnet Lundren are empty – the orchard, the willow on the riverbank, the dark hollows in the wood. The heat of the day seeps into him. He walks faster, seeking out hidden shade where they have never been, but where Drake might go – the cave at the shore end, the deepest passages through the gorse on the cliff path. He feels his pulse in his wing shoulder. Sweat drips down his bent back.

Gulls dip their arcs and rise above the glittering sea. Drake said to him once, 'There's nothing better than the deep dive, the swoop up through water like flight.' There is something far better, Verlyn wanted to say, thinking of Linnet Lundren. But he remembered the way Linnet looked at his beautiful brother.

He will find her. He will touch her with his one, strong hand, and show her he is more than feathers. He will tell her about the singing she makes in his bones.

The sun is beginning to dip. Werrity will be calling him in, finding his lean-to empty, tutting at the sky. Then Verlyn thinks of the darkest, coolest place there is on a summer's day, and despite the weary heat in his limbs he runs, along the cliff path, down to the shore, to the Webbe hut. The door is ajar. The pulse in Verlyn's shoulder quickens.

He nudges through the gap into the gloom, breathing in the stale oyster scent. Creels and oars are piled in corners. 'Linnet?' he whispers, but there is no one there in the dark.

His brothers have gone, but when he sits down on the warm stones by the hut he sees two shadows rise at the far end of the shore. They meander towards him. Their hands are joined. Every few paces they pause, their heads bending together. As they come closer, Linnet waves at him with the hand that is not clasped with Drake's.

'Idling today?' Drake says, and grins when Verlyn goes to meet them.

'I was looking for you.' Verlyn wishes for a shirt to cover his crooked body, his pale chest that folds inwards, wet with heat. He looks at Linnet. 'Not all Webbes have feathers,' he says.

Drake puts both his brown arms around Linnet's waist. 'No. And not all Webbes have wives. But Linnet will remedy that. Won't you?'

And while Drake smiles, Linnet kisses his cheek and says, right there before Verlyn, 'Yes.'

The heat in Verlyn's head, from the sun, from his sprint to the shore, becomes blinding. He begins to wade into the foamy sea.

'Not all Webbes can swim, either,' he hears Drake call, followed by Linnet's husky laugh.

He walks until he is thigh-deep in the water and drops backwards, the cold slapping into his neck. Sodden, his wing is heavy, dragging down against the rolling shingle. Not heavy enough. He floats in the lapping saltwater. It numbs the pain where the wing twists his shoulder.

Every morning, when he stands in his front yard and looks out at the sea, Verlyn Webbe counts his blessings. The first is his wife, Werrity. He is lucky to have kept her, all these years. He is grateful for the shirts and the coats she stitches him, looser in the sleeve now, to lessen the ache in his wing. The feathers have started to turn white. He does not mind that when a feather drifts to the floor of the house, Werrity pinches it up and drops it straight in the fire.

The next blessing he counts is his son, Marram. Barely a boy any more, his son is learning to dive, slowly lengthening his time underwater, growing his heart, stretching his limbs. His uncles have made a seventh seat in the stern of their boat. Sometimes Verlyn goes with them and watches Marram dive, wriggling like an eel away from the surface. The down at his thumbnail soaks away to nothing in the water. It makes Werrity smile to see her son salty, swaggering.

The last blessings Verlyn counts are his brothers, all six of them, stronger and braver and bigger of heart than he is. When the seven Webbes and their seven wives gather, Verlyn greets Linnet as if she had always been Linnet Webbe, the gleeful wife of his youngest brother, Drake. Linnet laughs as she leans as if to shake his hand, and instead grasps the feather tips that spring white from his coat sleeve. Then Verlyn clenches the one strong hand that never touched her, and gently pulls his wing away.

KITE

FIRWIT WAKES WITH HIS cheek hot against waxy sheepskin and remembers, as he rubs away the itch of it with his gnarled knuckles, that he is alone. His mind is slower now; it creaks in the mornings as his bones do, and it is only the feel of this sheepskin wad beneath his head that reminds him. He has burned the feather pillows, choking on their scorched smoke. In case of fever lurking there, he told himself. He did not believe, and still does not, Ivy Rincepan's words, the day she helped him clear the sickness from the room.

'Look close,' Ivy Rincepan said, dangling one of the pillows from her stubby fingers. All Firwit saw was a well-used sack of down, blotched brown. 'I can know who stuffed this from the jig-jag tacking and all the quills poking through, for want of soaping the inner. One of Guller's, done himself.' She tore at a loose corner, and pulled out a fistful of brown and grey down.

'He'll put any old flotsam in them. I daresay whatever he sweeps from his own floor. I opened up one I had off him, once, to put into fresh ticking, and found a lark's head amongst the down. My youngest had been talking in his sleep all winter and that were the reason.' Ma Rincepan poked about in her fist, sending curling drifts into the air. 'Here's one, see?' She picked out a straight grey quill. 'A flight feather, that is. Put those in your pillows and even the soundest mind won't rest. No sleep, not even for the blessed, with that under your ear. Guller knows that sure as anyone. Maybe it's carelessness, or meanness with his stuffing, but I see malice in it.'

Firwit did not see malice, for he was too weary to see anything at all at that moment. Then he saw only the tales of the village women, his neighbour Ma Rincepan among them; women who will find magic where there is nothing, and prefer gossip to good sense.

He is too old now for fancies, for dreaming. He burned the pillows only because he wanted them gone. But turning against his folded sheepskin at night now, for he will not take a new pillow, he dreams his brother, Murnon, over and over.

A cracked heel bone – a stumble in the sheep field, his first slip in fifty years – was all that kept Murnon in his bed at first. He was rueful. The sheep would keep, he said. But Murnon, his foot nestled in a pile of fleece, could no longer keep his nightly habit of walking out at the deepest hour. He lay awake, a fidgeting, twitching heap against the pillow. He'd never wanted more than a few hours' rest before the dawn, after he came home from his nightly ramble. But now that he must lie in bed, sleep was stolen from him.

A sickness only, a strange fever that would pass, Firwit thought, brought on by a split bone. So, he let in the night wind off the hill, hoping the brackeny air would bring Murnon peace. He warmed the hardened honey the beekeeper had brought and sweetened the last of the barley bread his brother had made, but Murnon would not take it. You eat, he said, and rubbed his reddened eyes. In the dark, Murnon whimpered, but when Firwit lit a candle for the comfort of light his brother snuffed it out, as if he knew, even then, it must not be used up.

After four days and nights of wakefulness, Firwit could no longer get sense from Murnon. After six, he barely recognised his brother. His haggard face became a wraith of its original, eyes shrunk deep in hollows dark as bruises. The voice that rasped from his parched mouth spoke in riddles, of stars and night, flight and wings, only halting now and then to beg for a sight of sky.

Firwit used strips from his own workshop, edge cuttings of sheepskin, to bind the mittens tight on his brother's hands, for after Murnon had plucked the lashes Firwit feared he'd tatter his very eyelids away.

Denied his night walks, his brother's mind had slipped away so fast that he chewed through the leather whenever Firwit gave in to sleep for an hour or two. Sleep, the gift he could not give his brother.

A fortnight it is now since Murnon took those chewed strips, hoarded for the purpose, and made one long cord. Plaited neatly, it had been, as if his fingers found calm at the end, as if his mind regained judgement and his wrecked body some unworldly strength. Firwit, waking to a chilly dawn, had taken a blanket to Murnon and stared, senseless, at the empty bed. His brother had not dragged himself far. The cord he'd made still held him, slumped against the ladder to the loft, and it was tough, too tough for Firwit's pocket knife, so Firwit hacked in panic at the leather and was not ready when the weight of the body dropped hard and threw him against the boards. The criss-cross pattern of the plaited leather stayed in the loose skin of Murnon's throat. Firwit covered the mark with his own best kerchief for the burying, in pity, in penance.

It is that moment, the struggle of his knife against the cord and the joined tumble of two old men against wood that hurt only one of them, which tosses Firwit from his sheepskin sleep each night. He bears the terror without the comfort of light, for he wants his share of darkness. It was Murnon made the candles from their own sheep's tallow, never Firwit. There are two left, pale guardians standing on the mantel, silent on the matter of how they came into being.

In the midnight black Firwit listens to his own fast breath like the ghost of his brother's in this room. Then he listens to the parchment in the windloft above his bed, the smooth, creamy skins of Murnon's sheep splayed in their frames, which shift and jolt against the beams in the night breeze. So unlike the sheep they came from, those thinned skins. They are like row upon row of ships' sails, catching the breeze through the latticed walls, longing to cut across water in full sun. The gentle clacks of the frames in the rush of air used to call him to a calm day's work of soaking, scraping, cutting. They sound to him like awkward wingbeats now. Is this what Murnon heard, a roof full of flapping birds above his sleepless head? Was it this, over a pillow stuffed with Guller's feathers, that made him walk out every night?

Firwit rubs his knuckles, stiff as untended hinges. When his fingers will bend he pulls on boots, fleece and cap, pushes the door and steps out into the quiet night. Its air is a sweet-salt draught of grass, first sap and seaweed. Bones aching, he lets the slope lead him further up the hillside, treading his path from the night before, the night before that. The sea hushes far below; it must be calm at the shore. The forest whispers back. He is the only restless one, out in the night.

Before the turn, before sleep left him altogether, Murnon was the night walker. Save the nights of the Great Storm, when trees slid across the hill, there's hardly been a midnight his brother did not slip out into the dark. He'd be out for hours, watching the sheep, watching what else? Firwit has not dwelt on it till now, now he is taking his turn in the night. He has come to think that this is where his brother left his spirit, in the dark on the hill, for he is sure it was not in his body that last week. The raging, weeping thing that half-resembled Murnon, writhing in its feather bed, did not know him, and he did not know it.

He climbs higher with the path, hearing scurries in the undergrowth, until in the moonlight he can see the stone wall of the sheep field above. The smell of their dung comes to him and is a comfort and a worry at once. He only understands these creatures as carcasses, can handle a flayed sheepskin with his eyes shut, but living, breathing in this field, they are Murnon's domain. Reaching the wall, he scans for the huddle of bodies, imagines them warm in their waxy coats. He would like to grasp those curls, like a human head, like his own before it withered to the whiskered scalp beneath his cap. Murnon's curls were white as sea foam by the end.

The sheep are at the high edge of the field, where the earth is driest, he supposes. Perhaps he can get to know their ways, get to grips with the work his brother did. He skirts the field outside the low stone wall, creeping towards them. His toes are dampening with the dew soaking his boots, the wind rushing louder on the hill, filling his ears with its low chords. He stops when he hears a high, mournful whistle floating in the currents above him. A shape circles against the ghostly cloud, then sweeps down to land on the top wall of the sheep field. Crows will peck the eyes from new lambs, Murnon has told him. But there are no lambs yet, and he knows that whistling song. It is no crow.

He walks towards the shape. When he raises a hand to pull his cap down tighter against the wind, it rises and swoops close over him, its piping wail threading through his head before it turns and flies off towards the forest. Firwit stares after it. That whistle is the call of a kite. Never has he heard one at night, but when has he listened? He knows from the hunters that kites sleep through the dark. The younger ones even lie down, like people in their beds.

There are still many hours before dawn will come and the night is chill, as if the moon's icy eye made cold where it spread its light. The sheep are quiet. Firwit unbends his creaking knees and begins to tramp again, along the ridge of the hill towards the wood. The ground drops down to the trees, where the wind cannot reach to whip at him. He steps between two trunks, into the wood's held breath, and stands. The quiet is like a blanket about his head. It is darker, the wood is fuzzed grey where moonlight reaches down between branches, and Firwit stalks slowly on his hidden feet, placing palms on trunks, soothed by the scent of bracken as he treads it down.

From deep in the wood, he hears the long, piping cry. He shakes his head to shake out the sound, but it comes again. He is careless of the brambles that tear at his legs, of the cracks of snapping deadwood as he pushes through the tangle, holding twigs from his eyes with his bent elbow. Moonlight pours into the clearing and he can see, in a wide patch that has been swept clean of leaf mulch, a dark thing, lying like a dropped shawl. He looks around at the still trees. Bending down close, he makes out that the thing is a large bird. It looks dead. He nudges it with a knuckle, then grasps a wing, the feathers seeming to thrust against his palm. He turns it over. It is not whole. There is no mound of chest, or soft belly feathers. Rather, it is the husk of a kite, no bones within, the inside of the skin rough but dry, hardened. Someone has made it, carefully peeled the skin from bird flesh, cleaned it, kept the feathers good. He thinks of Guller, the bird man, for who else would know, or want, to make such a thing? Firwit picks it up by the head and finds twists of wool stuffed inside. It is wool from Murnon's sheep. He knows by the feel of its waxy warmth, the spring of the curl.

All the walk home, the world is silent. Firwit carries the kite skin, the wind giving life to its wings even in his grasp. His thoughts drift with the whistle in the woods, the looping calls of kites woven together with his brother's cries. Murnon, Guller, birds where they should not be; there's no sense to it, and he feels the place where he keeps his brother in his mind grow dark. He cuts Murnon down from the ladder three, four, five times before he reaches home, where he tucks the bird husk under the rosemary bush in the yard before he opens the door. It does not belong in the house.

The parchment is silent in the windloft. It will soon be day.

After dozing through dawn's rustlings, Firwit wakes as he often does now, to a rap at the door and his name called, loud and cheery. Ivy Rincepan has taken to bringing him milk, and lately adding a loaf or a cake, of a morning. He watches her gaze flit around the smirched room when she sidles in.

Ivy Rincepan frowns. 'Don't you get worn, Firwit,' she says, as she clatters about. 'You get back to your habits, that'll set you right.' She passes him a cup of milk. 'Now drink up,' she says. 'I got by the dairy early, and March put cream in that for you, and all.'

He sits up, heavy, in his bed, and watches her. She is fishing now into the cold pot where yesterday he tried to boil the salt out of some cured mutton for supper, as Murnon used to do, but instead turned the meat to shoe leather.

'Three soaks, and change the water,' she says briskly, the grey strip dripping between her fingers. 'I'll take this one for the hound.'

Firwit's only skill with food is turning the sheep's soured milk into cheese, but the season is long over, and he's none left to trade. Bread and meat were Murnon's gifts, another thing he will have to learn. As if she sees his thought, Ivy goes on, 'I'm needing some good raw wool, myself. Enough for a dozen skeins or so, and the same again for Sil, up on the hill. Never puts down her knitting, that one. I know Murnon had a few sacks left to trade.' She is glancing at the stack of sacks, dry in the hearth corner. 'Keep you in milk and meat a good while on that. Eggs too, if you want, from the ducks. Better than those nest-robbed nothings Guller used to give your brother – barely a mouthful each one, and beaks sticking between your teeth.'

Firwit is grateful for the kindness. He nods and Ivy opens up a sack and begins pulling out handfuls of waxy curls, filling her basket. As it reaches brimful, Firwit again reaches the edge of his knowledge, which used to match so neatly with Murnon's that neither took any notice of where one stopped knowing and the other started. How much wool is a good trade, he cannot guess. How many eggs, how much meat, is a brimming basket worth?

Ivy closes up the sack and, rubbing her hands on her skirts, peers into the empty grate. 'And May the fiddle-master's after more of your fine parchment, now she's took to writing down her tunes. You'll have some ready for her soon, will you?'

Firwit is still clutching the cup of milk, not drinking though he is thirsty. He is thinking of the bird husk in the yard, the kite whistling in the forest. Ivy is staring at him, hands on hips. 'Must keep body and soul together, Firwit,' she says, stern as to a child, 'and the best way to keep whole is to keep at your work.' She nods up at the windloft, from where the faint tap of the parchment frames echoes.

As she bends to poke at the dead ashes, a feather slips from between the ceiling planks and drifts down to stroke Ivy's neck. She shrieks and bats blindly at it, but when she sees it is not a spider, or a moth wagging frantic wings, she is solemn.

'What's one like this doing here?' she asks Firwit. The feather is as long as her forearm, striped red. He can't answer. He works at keeping birds from the windloft, hooking down nests that sometimes sprout in the rafters. 'Not one as belongs in a house. You mark this, Firwit. The only man likely to have feathers like this about him is Guller, and you know where I believe he stands in all of this.'

Firwit's neck is hot against the sheepskin wad. Old ma's tales, he reminds himself, but the feather has irked him. It looks to be a kite's. He left the bird husk in the yard.

He climbs the ladder to the windloft when she has gone. The wind flicks the parchment skins in their frames, those taut white sails, and he walks between the rows, letting the breeze that has dried them cool the sweat on his neck. The wind is soft today through the loft's open sides, the lattice of beams there casting stripes of shadow across the skins. They are sleek, unblemished, every one scalded and scraped in the good calm of work that Firwit used to find so easily. He crouches in the shady space between the frames and picks up a long feather, reddish brown. Another lies in the next row, turning in the draught. He looks up for nests, even though he knows Ivy Rincepan was right. These are no eave-birds. The long whistle of the kite on the hill, and its reply caught in the deep net of the forest, echoes in his head.

It is Murnon's flock that gave the hides, Murnon's skill with a knife that split them, so cleanly, that each hide yielded two faultless sheets. At the loft's far end is the last skin, the one he's yet to work at. When it is finished, there will be nothing to do but take up Murnon's knife and begin learning how to slaughter, how to bleed, and finally, how to flay. Murnon's blade is long, heavy, petering to a fine point. Firwit picks up his own blade, a dull crescent moon; feels the sweep and arch of the scraping work in his shoulder. He tests the curved metal edge with his thumb. He has done half of everything for more than forty years.

He puts the blade back up on its hook and carries the two feathers down from the windloft and out into the yard. He cannot remember which of them, himself or Murnon, hammered down the stones that shine now in the places they've trodden most. He scans the lane below and then ducks to look beneath the rosemary bush. The bird skin has gone. Carried away by a fox, of course, or one of the village dogs. But it is Ivy Rincepan's warning he cannot shake from his mind as he lies back down on his bed. He's not spoken to Guller for many years. It was Murnon did any trades they might need with him. Firwit, ever hearing the man's shrill laugh in the ale room or on the lane, would turn away. There was something in Guller's childlike face, some darkness behind it, that he could not abide.

Firwit sleeps, deep and dreamless against his sheep-skin, until dusk. Later, when the bats begin to sweep the insects from the gloom, he sets off again, up the hill, letting the wind fill his ears.

At the sheep field, he sits in the nook Murnon built into the wall for the purpose, the stone pressing into his spine, and waits. When the piping call of the kites begins, he follows the sound in his mind, its threads spooling over and round and down to the wood. But pushing once more through the wood's spindles and sweet bracken, he finds the clearing empty. They are leaves, not feathers, that rustle and rise around his boots. Only as he is tramping home in the rug-thick dark before dawn does he hear the faintest wheeling cry behind him.

It is up to the windloft he goes in the first morning light. Long feathers litter the floor, turning, red and silver-grey. He gathers them up, feels them resist his clutch as they pulse in the breeze.

His head is furred with lack of sleep. His bones feel weak. Ivy Rincepan will not come knocking yet, and it is for the comfort of the familiar arch and sweep that he takes his crescent blade from its hook and begins to work at the last skin. The long rasps as he scrapes are like breaths. He sees Murnon lying in his feather bed, his eyes red raw, his skin faded to ash. Still he scrapes, long slow sweeps across the skin. When his arm is tired, he changes hands and scrapes the other way, but still no calm. He drops the blade, picks up the bag where he has stuffed the feathers and climbs back down, his hands shaky on the ladder.

Firwit's knuckles are hardened wax again when he raps at Guller's door, which is streaked in green-grey ridges. Above the door, a frame the shape of a small crooked house is built into the wall in place of a lintel. Inside the crooked house, caged by iron spindles, a magpie rattles back and forth. He's seen this before, as a child, when the first fowl-monger lived here. The magpie hunts for the way out, not understanding what it is to be caught, no notion of a trap.

As the door swings open a rancid stink hits him, of bird grease and feathers scorched in the grate.

Guller's black eyes stare up at him. He is no taller than a child, and his smile is childish, gap-toothed.

'Ah! Fine to see you, Firwit the parchment man. Come in, come in.' His voice is wheedling.

'Let that sorry prisoner out,' Firwit replies, nodding up at the scuttling magpie, and waits for Guller's shrill laugh to be over before following him inside.

A string of songbirds, tied like onions, hangs drying above the hearth. There are feathers everywhere, stuck in cobwebs, drifting like thistledown on the floor. A white goose lies on the table, each wing severed and fanned, held outspread by a peeled branch tied along its length. The goose's eyes follow Firwit as he steps around the room.

'What use would a bird skin be?' Firwit asks. He does not want to breathe this foul air long.

'Where shall I begin, parchment man? A wren skin for luck at sea. A rook skin for stealth. A swallow skin to dry a drunk.'

'A kite skin.'

'Ah! Those high-sky spirits.' Guller's eyes dart and flash. His grin reveals sharp yellow teeth. 'You hear them, up on the hill?'

'I believe that's where they belong,' Firwit says.

'And that's where you found those, eh?' Guller is looking at the reddish spears that poke from Firwit's sack.

'These I found in the house.'

'What luck you have. Brought them for me, have you? I'll do you a good trade for those.' Guller scoops from a pocket a fistful of tiny eggs, blue, brown and white, some speckled, not two the same among them, and holds them up to Firwit. 'Shouldn't find beak nor bone in there,' he says, 'but they'll make breakfast either way.'

'A kite skin,' Firwit repeats. His jaw is tight.

'Good for flying, I'd say.' Guller laughs, looking sidelong at Firwit. 'So high they fly, those sky spirits. You hear them, even when you can't see them.' He begins to whistle, that same looping, wavering note that spins in the darkness above the sheep field and into the wood. Guller's eyes are closed. He begins to sway and drift around the room, singing, whistling, as if the spirit of a kite were in his mouth.

The smog of the room is caught in Firwit's throat. He grips his bag of feathers and stares at the goose on the table, its wings outstretched beside it. The dark red spots on its sides have spread.

'A kite skin, Guller, with my brother's wool tucked inside.' Firwit's voice croaks. 'I had it. Now it's gone.'

The whistle has carried Guller in his dance to a dark corner. He shakes something out, making dust rise, and brings to Firwit the hollow bird he carried from the hill.

'Yours now, then, parchment man,' he says, and holds it out. 'It was Murnon's. I made it for him myself, when he asked.'

'What for?' Firwit grasps the wings, feels again the strength in them, the force of taut feathers.

Guller grins and lets out a curling note between his teeth.

'Good for flying, like I said. Lifting the spirits. You put your mind to it – and Murnon could – or, you put your mind in it.' Guller nods at the skin. 'Only takes this, and a little wanting, a little bite of a red-top agaric, chewed up. See the stars from up there, kite-wise. Anyone can do it. All sorts do. You ask them, those that come to the wood. I've had Quayle the fiddler up there, little Gertrude Quirk, that lovely Madden from the stables. All as high and happy as kites.'

Firwit turns the bird skin and pokes his finger into the pinch of Murnon's wool beneath the scalp.

'Sky spirit, your brother. Lover of stars.' Guller's eyes no longer flash. 'Come yourself, to the woods one night,' he calls, as Firwit opens the door and leaves the rattle of magpie in its cage behind him.

Firwit lies down on his bed with the bag of feathers stuffed beneath his head. *Flying*, Guller said. *A sky spirit, your brother. Come yourself.* He knew Murnon by day, sheep-tender, bread-baker. He did not know him by night.

He twists and turns, searching for Murnon in the reddish dark behind his eyelids. He senses the answer is out there, in the dark, in Guller, but he cannot follow his brother there. Flight feathers, they are, inside the sacking, but it is only the quills poking through that keep him from sleep. Perhaps it does not matter, the dark space in his mind where Murnon sits.

At dawn, the wind rises and the parchment frames clatter in the windloft, until Firwit climbs the ladder, squinting in the bright stripes of light.

The skin he meant to finish leans up against the lattice, lit from behind, and he sees that with his scraping, the sweep of one hand and then the other, he has thinned out shapes like two curving wings. With his short cutting knife, he slices through the parchment skin. He needs only a length of twine then; a few stitches. As he works, the last dots of down that have followed him from Guller's house lift from his shirt and are carried out through the open eaves and lost.

He climbs the hill in the clear midday light. The sheep look up from grazing when he reaches the wall.

He does not know whether they sleep at night, or only rest sometimes, when the world wearies them. He tucks the kite skin between the stones around the flat seat of the wall nook, and then in the white daylight he sits, the waxen white curls of the sheep below him, the deep white ruffs of cloud above, the cut parchment pale in his hands. When a kite's whistle streams from far above, it is as it should be: the sound of the hill, with the chit of the birds in the undergrowth and the hiss of the insects in the grass.

Firwit lets the evening lull him, but when the first bats come to cut through the dark he is alert. With the night, the wind grows stronger, the sounds of the hill are washed away, and he unwinds the twine across his lap, his fingers slow from stillness. There are no stars to be seen, but a smudge of cloud is brightened by the moon buried deep behind it: his brother's night sky to fly in. He clambers up to stand on the seat, the twine-end between his teeth. Then he hurls the parchment up and the wind takes it, flies it fast and spreads its wings white and high above Firwit's head. It wheels and settles into a rising, falling flight, the tug of the twine sending throbs into his hands. When, soon, the eerie whistle of the kites pours up from the wood, Firwit listens as the parchment bird, with no need of feathers, is woven in the silver threads of their sound.

A WINTER GUEST

B Y NIGHTFALL, EVERYONE KNEW the man's
name was Redwing. The fishers saw him first, dragging his boat up on to the shore. They were sitting out the
last day of November in their huts, as was custom. As was
custom, they herded the stranger to the ale room. Soon
a crowd was spilling out of the door and into the dunes.

'Gossip is, he's a fine one,' said Gad, when she came
knocking on Clotha's window. 'And a head taller than
any of them. Hair like a bonfire. I want a look.'

Clotha laughed at her friend. 'What good will it do
you?'

'Oh, a dream.' Gad smiled. 'Not just for me.' She
squeezed Clotha's waist as she pulled her away along
the path by the fishers' cottages.

'I'll wait outside,' Clotha said.

But Gad kept hold of her as they nudged through
the villagers, milling in the dunes despite the pinch of

November wind at their cheeks, and she held on even tighter as she steered Clotha in through the ale room door. 'Redwing,' she whispered, and they craned past heads and shoulders to where the gleaming man sat.

The room was thick with voices, and all faces were turned towards him as he looked about and nodded and smiled. Even May the fiddler, churning out a jig in the corner, kept her eyes on him as she played. Clotha noticed his crooked teeth, the line that creased one cheek. Still, he was horribly handsome. He looked up then and caught her eye. His sideways gaze was so long it made Clotha blush.

'Told you,' Gad said, when she passed her a cup. 'Look at those fiery locks.'

'Who's misty-eyed?' said Clotha.

'But married.' Gad's sigh was longer than usual.

'A good thing too.' Clotha felt Gad clutch her hand, the way she did each time they silently remembered that she had been married too, once. The imprint of Gad's hand stayed so long that she didn't feel her friend slip from her side.

Clotha had reached the last dune, chasing after Gad, when she felt the thud of steps behind her.

'Your friend said you might have a bed for the night,' the gleaming man said.

'And you've had no other offers?' Clotha kept walking. He matched her pace, and gave her that sidelong look again. 'Redwing?' she said. He held out a hand. When her palm met his, he turned it upwards to his lips. *The tide takes, the tide brings in*, she said to herself. *Why shouldn't a sea widow make her own catch?* and she took him home.

A warm scent of pepper came into the house with him. She did not ask where he had come from, in his boat, whether all the men and women there were as tall and broad and burnished as he. With their joined hands they pulled each other closer behind Clotha's door. It was true, his kiss was such deep relief, her mouth watered. Two years; four and twenty months, she had been alone. How many nights? She counted only the treads of the staircase as they flew over them. Gad knew Clotha had only one bed.

When she woke, Clotha rubbed her eyes. Then she touched the russet fringe of the man's eyelashes. She kissed them, but he did not stir. Away she crept.

A December dawn flushed deep at the windows. When she stepped outside, barefoot and naked but for a blanket, the cold spun pleasure across her skin.

She took tea upstairs, but still Redwing slept. She blew on his ears, she bit his thumbs; she reached chilled hands under the quilt and stroked. He only sighed and rolled his head on the pillow, flame hair sliding.

At noon, fierce with lust, she pulled the sheets right off him. 'Aren't you hungry?' she demanded.

'Yes,' Redwing said, his eyes aglow. 'Come back to bed.'

Clotha left the sheets in a puddle on the floor. She did not hear the knocking at her window below. There was nothing but Redwing's whispers, his pepper scent filling the room, all that day and into the night.

The next morning when she came downstairs, there was Gad, sitting at her table, hugging a loaf of bread.

'Brought you this,' Gad said, though she didn't let go. 'You didn't come to the workshop yesterday.'

'He's still here,' Clotha said.

'I guessed.' Gad narrowed her eyes. 'Where's he from, then?'

'I don't know. I don't care! We've hardly left the bed,' Clotha whispered, watching Gad tear a lump from the loaf and chew on it.

'Well, come back soon. It's dull without you to talk to.'

'There's always your mother,' said Clotha.

'Sil? Not this time of year. Out wandering in the fog all day. And anyway, I do want to hear.' They both looked up at the ceiling, picturing the bed beyond.

'Clotha,' came Redwing's voice down the stairs. 'I miss you.'

Gad grinned. 'I'll let myself out.'

'Like you let yourself in,' said Clotha.

'Just like that.'

As soon as the door had slammed shut behind Gad, Clotha took the loaf and ran up the stairs three at a time.

After a week, there was no food left in the house.

'I'll go,' she said to Redwing between kisses, peeling herself from the bed.

'I'll stay,' he murmured in her ear.

She walked light-headed through the village, until she found herself at the workshop door. The ring of chisels, hammers and planes gave her a pang.

Inside, Gad did not look up when Clotha stood beside her. 'It's been more than a week,' she said, and gouged harder at the wood on the workbench.

'If it weren't for you, I wouldn't have him at all,' said Clotha. 'I'll be back, soon.'

'Don't hurry on my account. One carving each, we've to do for the year-turning fair, and you've hardly begun yours.'

'I'm busy,' said Clotha, but she watched her friend's fingers with envy as they ran along the woodgrain.

Gad looked up at her. 'You said it was for Madden, too. Since she won't do one this year.'

'Please don't talk about my sister now,' Clotha said, and she headed for the door.

At the dairy, when Clotha asked for milk and cheese, the dairywomen March and Iska stopped their work so they could nudge each other.

'Keeping him all to yourself?' Iska blurted, as she handed over the goods.

'He needs rest,' Clotha lied.

'I'll bet he does,' said March as she turned back to the butter churn.

At the shore, Gill Skerry the fisher was gruff. 'Enough for two,' he said, as he slapped a pair of mackerel into Clotha's hands.

By the time she got home, she wasn't hungry at all. As she opened the door, she breathed in the peppery smell and found Redwing standing there, washed and dressed. 'What, are you leaving?' she asked.

'Oh no,' he said, 'I was coming to find you. You took so long.' He lifted her hands high and ran them for her through his tangled hair, and there was no time to eat or to say there were things she ought to do, outside of the bed.

That night, Clotha plotted. Since Redwing slept until noon or longer, and could not be roused, she would creep out to the workshop early each morning. She would finish her carving for year-turning, and be back before he missed her. It was for her sister too, after all. The thought kept her awake, the joy of working the wood again, rough in her hands, bending to her own shape, while she stood beside Gad at the bench.

But when dawn came, Redwing's eyes opened. He pressed close to her on the pillow, solemn.

'There's something I must tell you, Clotha,' he said.

She did not go to the workshop.

'Three months,' she told Gad, when, a week later, she stood beside again her at the workshop bench. The carvings had sprung into life, beasts of the sea and air and earth. Her own cut of wood stood under a dusty piece of sacking in the corner.

'If you came back now, you'd have time to finish it,' Gad said, when she saw her glance at it. 'And why three months?'

'He didn't say.'

'You didn't ask?'

'What can I do?' said Clotha. 'He's happy there.'

'Are you?' Gad's grey eyes were stern. 'You'll come to the year-turning fair, even if your carving doesn't?'

'I'll try. It's hard to get away.'

'You look thin,' Gad called after her as she left. Clotha dawdled on the lane, reluctant to meet the glares at the dairy and on the shore.

'I know nobody here,' Redwing said when she told him about the fair, the carvings, the fire, the merry downing of ale. 'Won't it be odd, to dance with strangers?'

'You're not a stranger to me,' Clotha pleaded. 'I'll dance with you all night, I promise.'

'All right,' he said, and he kissed her before she could say any more.

But when the day came, Redwing could not let her alone even long enough to get dressed. 'I'm more hungry for you than ever,' he said, and pulled her skirt from her hips. 'Don't make me share you. We've only two months now.'

Clotha gave in to his hands and his lips. Two months, and what then? A part of her sighed, drinking in the promise of a silent house, an empty bed, the tap of Gad's knuckles at the window. It was not so far away.

January brought snow upon snow, sealing them into the house. Clotha came up with errands to run. 'I have to help clear the lanes,' she said. 'It's the custom here, in winter.' But she snuck away from the scrape of shovels and tramped up the hill, with only the sound of her boots for company. The air was fresh as water. She gulped it deep and cold in her lungs.

'I have to help chop wood for the elder folk,' she said.

'It's the custom here, is it? If you say so,' said Redwing. 'I'll keep the bed warm for you.' And he rolled away, showing her his long, freckled back.

Clotha lingered in the icicled woods until dusk closed the branches in. How quiet, how still, the stars were where they showed. She thought of her big sister, Madden, staring out at them from their bed when they were children.

When she set off home she walked the long way round, taking the path near Gad's house. By the glowing window she crouched and heard angry voices, a chair scraping stone. She peered inside and saw Gad and her husband, yelling at each other across the table. Gad said something she couldn't hear, and then the shouts turned to laughter, somehow, until they were hooting and Gad's arm was around her husband's shoulder.

'We've had not a harsh word,' Clotha said to Redwing, when he embraced her at the door.

'Why would I be anything but kind to you?' he asked.

'Kindness has many forms,' she said, but he squeezed her tighter, and longer, until she did not have the breath to say more.

The thaw came early, in February. Clotha's fingers fiddled. Her feet tapped. She itched to start digging, turning the earth, making good for new growth.

'But my love, we've only a month,' said Redwing when he found her pulling garden tools from the lean-to. 'Come back in the warm.'

February was the shortest month, at least. She began cooking stews for Redwing that took hour upon hour of stirring. She stripped the bed and boiled up the sheets until the windows dripped, then hung them out in the rain.

Each morning while Redwing slept until noon, stretched out in the bed that now felt like his, Clotha tiptoed about the garden, forking the earth half-heartedly. She left the door wide open to wash out the peppery fug that filled her nostrils. Then she sat at the table, drinking up her own stillness. She conjured Gad in the chair across from her, gnawing on lumps from a loaf, grouching about her husband.

One morning, Redwing woke with her at dawn again. There was only a week of February left. His hair had grown so long it spread across the pillow in a fiery flood. His eyes were solemn.

'Clotha,' he said. 'I'm so sorry I have to leave. But I've decided. I will come back next winter. I will steer my boat to you, my love, and we will have each other, in this blissful bed, for three months more.'

Clotha stretched her lips into a smile.

When he dozed again, she was out of the house in less than a breath, stomping through mud that splattered her legs, up the hill until she was standing outside Gad's house. Nobody answered her knock, so she let herself in. She paced about on the cold stone floor, round and round the table, back and forth at the window, until finally she saw Gad's face frowning in at her.

'Had enough?' she said, and dumped her basket on the table.

'He's leaving.'

'Thank the stars,' said Gad, as she pulled out her packages. She handed Clotha the loaf.

'Can I stay, just until he's gone?' Clotha asked, when they'd eaten half the bread.

'It's my fault he's there,' said Gad, tearing another piece.

'It's even worse. He said he'll come back. Next year.'

Gad laughed until she was choking on crumbs. 'You're welcome in my house, always. You know that,' she said. 'But you should go to say goodbye, at least.'

'To be sure that he's really left?'

'I would. Now eat up. You're a will-o'-the-wisp.'

On the last day of November, Clotha was already at her window when Gad knocked. Gad was waddling now, her belly so round and taut that when Clotha pressed her palm to it, she felt the baby kicking inside.

'They're saying there's a man arrived, at the shore,' Gad puffed. 'I'm going to take a look.'

'I'll lock the door,' said Clotha.

'I would.'

Clotha sat at her table, breathing the air that smelled only of her house, and the faint trace of bread Gad had left behind. While she waited, she planned carvings she might make this year, beasts of the sea and earth and air.

After a while, there was a scratching at the door, not like the thundering knock Gad used. She slid under the table, where she could not be seen. The scratching stopped. She waited and waited. Then she heard footsteps, a woman's voice and, answering, unmistakable, Redwing's deep tones. There was a pause, before two sets of footsteps pattered away down the path.

'He's gone,' Gad yelled through the window before she came inside, and lowered herself into a chair. She thumped a large cheese on to the table.

'What was that?' Clotha asked.

'That was Iska, works at the dairy.' Gad broke the cheese and shoved a huge piece into her mouth.

'Go on,' said Clotha.

Gad chewed and chewed. 'Iska didn't get one glimpse of Redwing last year, and didn't she let us know it, whinging on and on every time I went for milk. So, I told her this was her chance. We came past your house, and I stood there and watched her stride up to him on your doorstep, brazen. He kissed her hand when she held it out.'

'As fine as ever?'

'Oh yes. Iska thought so. The last I saw she was leading him back along the river path.'

'Iska and Redwing,' Clotha smiled. 'What can I do to thank you?'

Gad pushed the cheese towards her. 'Have some,' she said.

TURNING

ICE HAS CRACKED. SNOW melt has slid from trees to swell the muddy earth. First shoots have risen, and beech sap has burst into shrill green leaves. The boy, Finch, picks his way through last year's rusty bracken, making for the wood. He carries a fiddle, and the weight of a promise sworn: he is to practise all morning, far from the house, until the scrape of bow on string becomes a tune.

In the wood, the melodies belong to birds. The boy listens to their leaping notes. About him, the waking trees stretch. Dark moss springs between their toes. He shins up on to the shoulders of an oak. He feels its limbs lift him as he hunts for early nests. Birds flit wild-eyed to where the new green shade is deepest, and the fiddle lies, forgotten, below.

The boy's pockets are plump, eggs nestled in dry leaves. He reaches a glade, where the ground is furred with yellow grass. A tree stands in the middle, broken-limbed, stunted, but lush with ivy. Two wrens dart from its shadows, the tick-tick-tick of their warning call filling the green air. They flee and leave the clearing in the silent stillness of a stopped clock.

The boy creeps around the ivied trunk, ready to dig for hidden nests. Leaf skeletons lie like hardened snow-flakes among the sleeping roots. He bends to pick one up and finds the root beneath is warm. It is a gnarled foot. He jerks his hand away and stumbles back, heart drumming. The tree is hollow, arched like a doorway on the sunlit side. There inside it, garlanded with leaves, stands an old man. His hair is ringlet moss, his skin the weathered grey of winter oak leaves. He holds out his arms. His upturned palms glisten. Droplets hang in his curling beard. His eyes are filled with cloud.

The boy watches as a bee circles the man's head and lands on his cheek. Another wriggles up his neck. Another fumbles at his wrist. As the bees rise and return, calling in their drowsy humming song, they bring others. The old man's palms are soon dotted with their small brown bodies, ambling, busying. Slowly he turns his hands and cups them together, a bowl of thanks with bees inside.

The old man begins to walk. The boy follows him from the glade and hops close by him through the wood. His feet are quick beside the man's slow steps. The old man pauses when trees block his path before trailing round them, left, right, lifting his feet high over bramble and fallen branch. Where his soles have printed, woodlice scurry and earwigs waggle their heads into the air.

The wood folds shut behind them. They pass through a gap in a crumbled wall and into the roofless remains of a cottage, burned down long ago. The boy has heard the tale of the witch who lived here once. His aunt, Gertie, loves to tell it hunched beside the fire. There's no trace of fire here now. Sunlight warms the weathered stones where lichen blotches gold and blue. An upturned basket sits in the nook where once there was a hearth. The old man crouches, his cloudy eyes gazing up into the sky. When he opens his cupped hands, bees flow like treacle towards the hole at the basket's edge. They pour inside and are gone. The man sits back on his haunches and licks one palm, then the other. He wipes his knuckles over his cheeks and licks again.

'Honey,' the boy says.

The old man nods. 'Will be. But you've a long wait yet. Fetch me that bowl on the wall there.' When the boy brings it, the man reaches out with fumbling fingers until he finds water, dips, washes.

'Will you give me some?'

'What do I get in return?'

The boy fumbles the fiddle to his chin. 'Play you a tune,' he says, and plucks at the strings.

'Not for me,' the old man says. 'The wood's own music is kinder to my ears.'

'An egg, then.' The boy picks one from his pocket and rolls it in the old man's palm.

'Thrush,' the old man says. 'Stealing their treasures?'

'You steal bees.'

The old man laughs, a flutter deep in his throat. The curls of his beard twist. When he hands back the egg there is an ant running down his forearm, following the winding paths of ridged green veins. 'What's your name?'

'Finch.'

'A fine name for an egg thief. You'll have honey if you earn it, Finch. If you take the time.'

The stopped clock of the glade is whirring now. The boy can hear it inside the basket of bees where he presses his ear.

Wind scurries new petals across hillsides. Wood pigeons puff and court. Rabbits pause to warm in noonday sun, and the birds make a choir of the deep green wood. As sun and cloud sweep the sky, the boy learns to catch bees. He does not need to smear last year's honey on his face and hands like the old man, for he can find the bees by sight, but he chooses to learn this way all the same. They stir rosemary and clover into old honey and set out for places by water, by blossom. The waterfall in the wood, the orchard by the river, they make their daylong home.

The boy learns to sit, honey-coated, neither twitching nor scratching, until the music of the woods and fields fills his ears. Blackbird melodies slow and echo inside his throat. The hiss of insects, the twang and whisper of trees, the beat of rabbits' feet, all play above the droning tune of the bees.

As blossom blows and the hedgerows turn from hawthorn white to fuchsia red, he carries the baskets of bees up to the headland, following the old man through the gorse maze to where the yellow flowers run thickest amongst the thorns. He watches the bees at each new spot, the dip and dance of flower heads, the windblown flight to and from the baskets.

'It's a dance they do in there, too,' the old man says. 'No need for fiddle tunes. There's sweeter music here than any scratched from a fiddle.' The hands he lays on the hives are growing more bent, twisted as roots, the nails like trapped flints. Where the bees have stung him there are bumps like barley grains under his wrinkled skin. The old man never grumbles, though these bumps grow, hardening, yellowing.

The boy learns to still his heart, with his ear against the basket weave, and hear in the bees' song what they will do. The hives and their golden load, the bees that dance and sing, are precious treasures. He calms the bees with smoke pressed from puffballs, or trickled from kindling. He is proud and pleased to have felt no stings.

The barley in the fields fattens and leans towards the moon. Mice scurry in its maze, their trails mapped in the starry sky by the sweep of owls. Beside the tumbledown cottage, petals drop from poppies on the witch's grave.

While the bees make frantic flights to summer's last blooms, the old man's eyes fill up with cloud as deep as a snowy sky. He speaks less and less, but sings back to the birds in the wood where he wanders, each step like shifting stones. His clothes are torn to leaf-shred by a season's weathering, the skin beneath his shirt a landscape of wrinkled leather. When they sit together amongst the baskets, the boy watches the slow throb in those thick green veins that have webbed the old man's arms and hands.

'Patience,' the old man says, as the boy listens to the whirring clocks of the hives, busier, faster. He feels the hum deep inside his ear, a sound like honey.

Swallows gather and suddenly are gone. Crab apples bulge and drop in perfumed carpets. Leaves fly across the low-lit sky, gold and brown, and sloes make purplish mist of the blackthorn bushes. The old man, stiffened in the chill of autumn's breath, talks of fire.

'No more time,' he says, amongst the baskets. 'You've earned your honey.' His voice creaks. He scratches at the barley grains beneath his skin, his mouth bent in a grimace.

At dusk, inside the haggard ruin of the cottage, the boy sets a small blaze, making a ring of flame around a flat stone. He remembers the witch in Aunt Gertie's story. When the fire is crackling, hot-bright, he does as the old man tells him and drops on dead leaves. Wind billows the smoke, and moths mingle with flying ash. The old man stands in the broken cottage doorway, a dark shape rooted in the smoke.

'Take one, Finch,' he says, a crooked finger pointing to the row of baskets by the wall. 'Put it straight on the stone.'

The boy shields his eyes against the fire's sparks. 'But the bees.'

'Winter's coming. They've done their work. Only way to get the honey.'

The boy waits for the old man to laugh, but he is silent. Moths flood up around his head and flicker in the smoke.

'I won't burn them,' the boy says. He hears the wheeze of the old man's breath as he wades now towards the baskets, the effort of lifting each foot like pulling stones from turf. He picks up a basket and leans over the fire to drop it on the glowing stone. The boy trembles as he watches flames lick up around the weave. The willow becomes a web of glow. Bees rage from the hole in its side. They spin in the smoke, hurling themselves at the old man, dropping into the flames. Their sound is like a scream in the boy's ears. The crackle of burning bodies makes his skin prick and he swipes at the smoke around his head, then feels the rich ache of a single sting on his neck.

Around the remaining baskets bees hang in the air, drowsy with smoke. The boy bends over them, touching the weave, feeling for the hum. He will not let them burn. He turns and stands, ready to defend his treasure.

The old man has scooped the combs from the fire stone and holds them out in his hands. Smoke ebbs and blooms in the wind through the broken cottage walls. The boy edges closer, his eyes on the strange pocked mounds of comb. His urge is to dash them to the ground, but they are too beautiful. He glances at the old man's face. His eyes are shut. His hair and beard whorl in ringlets that reach into the smoke like grasping ivy. The last shreds of his ruined shirt have withered like dead leaves and his dark skin is deeply lined, shrunk hard in furrows over bone and sinew. The bees that clung to him as their basket burned are dropping away, and the boy can see the barley-grain bumps of old stings. He watches as they split and burst out bud and tendril, white stars of flowers on vines that twine across ribs, furl around arms. Petals drop. Seeds fly in the darkening smoke. The creeping coat of leaves entangles wrists and fingers. It twists up to knot with hair and beard. From the old man's open mouth, more tendrils turn.

The boy runs in a stumbling sprint through the wood and does not stop until he finds the glade. The only whirr is inside him, the thrum of his heart, the hum in his blood. He touches the sting on his neck and stares at the wood's bare branches, his feet deep in the tangled roots of the hollow tree.

Time slows with his pulse. A chill creeps from the wood's shadows and into his bones. While it numbs him, the leaves of oak and beech sigh to the ground and curl. Bracken droops, and bramble sinks to earth. The boy wakes, shivering, and finds his way by grey moonlight between the trees. Ash has blown white across the grass before the cottage wall. Inside is moonlit stone and shadow.

Ice has cracked. Snow melt has slid from trees to swell the muddy earth. The boy, Finch, hugs a rug around him on the hearth. All winter he has practised at his fiddle, and now the tunes come easily. He has visited his aunt Gertie and played them for her, by her own fire. Now he watches ash flakes fly through the flames and away up the chimney, the ghosts of a thousand bees.

Frost shrinks away and the scent of rotten leaves rises around the dripping thatch. The boy walks from the house amongst birds dipping for twigs and moss, their chirrups bright as the spring sunlight, and follows them to where they are busy building nests. The ivy has crept and covered the tumbled cottage stones by the wood, making glossy banks of leaves. Sun warms the boy's skin. He scratches the bump like a barley grain that still itches on his neck, and ducks through the gap in the wall.

A tree stands amidst the ivy, one branch outstretched, tender new growth fanning from its crown. It is both old and new, its riven bark breaking here and there to let out budding shoots, lush with sap. The boy turns about it once, and touches the branch, cool against his palm. One day, he knows, he'll make his own fiddle, like the apprentices before him. He will claim this wood, cut it and bend it until it will play its own tune.

Behind the tree, the old cottage hearth is grown over. It is too early for eggs, but he parts the leaves to look for where the nests are growing, little cups lined with feather. Behind the ivy he sees the baskets piled in the nook. He bends away the twines and pulls one out. Husks of bees drift in the bottom beneath the comb, still heavy with wax.

The boy carries the basket into the wood, threading between cold trunks, lifting his feet high over bramble and mossy root. Birds chatter, flitting from branch to branch. The trees drip and creak.

When he reaches the glade he stands before the hollow tree, its bent limbs spun with clematis and ivy. A blackbird startles and swoops away. The wood ticks, and trees turn. He breaks open the comb from inside the basket, digs out clots of last year's honey and spreads them on his palm.

It is warm in the tree's hollow, where the wind cannot reach. The sunlight glows behind his eyelids. With one arm outstretched, his handful of honey a bowl of thanks, he waits to feel the drone of a bee crossing the glade. Ivy curls about his feet and catches at his skin. He scratches his neck where the bump still itches, until under his fingernail is a crescent of green sap. He feels the blackbird's song in his throat, and breathes in the damp scent of waking trees.

As twists of shrill green leaf unfurl and bracken spreads green light on the ground, he hears the whirr of a bee circling his head. Others land to browse his arms and palms. He lets them crawl, his eyes turned up to watch the flying clouds.

TETHER

LISTEN, FOR THE BEAT that runs through the gorse maze. It is an early twilight, the opening between last sun and first star, the door of the day closing until, soon, night will seal it shut. There are feet thudding in the gorse's winding tunnels, hearts thumping in time. The girls of Neverness are running the paths, the strings of their bows held taut in outstretched hands, their arrows trembling. Each has only one arrow, a ribbon tied to its tail, the silken band stitched with her own name.

Among the beating feet, Orta runs. She is a dumpling of a girl, taking her first turn at the gorse-maze game. The dress Gad made for her is too long, and the loose linen catches on thorns as she hurtles round corners, where the last of the gorse's flowers speckle yellow. The cap her grandmother knitted has already been plucked from her head as she ducked through a scratching arch. Here and there she passes other girls, their bows held high, their faces fierce. Orta may be smallest, but she is wilful. She will spear her arrow deep into the gorse, and lodge it amongst the thickest parts. She will have the reddest kiss, from a boy who has dived so deep for her arrow that his lips have been pricked into a bloody pincushion.

Look now, down the slope of the headland, to where the villagers of Neverness are gathered. Men and women are lighting torches from the bonfire, wandering together in the heather, their faces lit bright in the spreading dark. They are hungry for this year's gorse-burning, but they must wait: for the youngsters to play their game and be paired, one boy for each girl, one kiss for each ribbon. Many remember Crab Skerry, the boy lost in the burning. This time they will count them off, their sons and daughters, before they start their blaze.

Gad tucks a stray wisp of misty shawl around her mother as they watch for Orta to come pelting from the maze. They share the glow from their torch with Verlyn Webbe, too old now to carry his own with one hand. Verlyn gazes at his son, Marram, who is handing out scallops scorched on sticks in the bonfire. Marram's wife, Iska, shakes her head at the scallop he offers, her eyes fixed on the headland where her twin daughters are running through the gorse with their bows. Marram tickles her chin with the single feather that sprouts from his thumb.

Weaving about the heather, the folk of Neverness wait for the stars to prickle out. May the fiddler sways near the flames to warm her fingers as she plays her mournful tunes. The villagers have learned not to ask for a jollier jig from her. Away from the fire, near the path, Hark Oxley stands alone. He is a grown man now, in middle age, his face weather-creased, his hands roughened by stone. He bends to tousle the head of a sheepdog that bounds up to him. Following behind, slow on his ancient legs, is the dog's owner, Firwit. Hark greets the old man, and helps him to a tree stump to sit.

'I see Redwing's back for another winter,' Firwit says, and nods towards a tall man whose long hair is lit red by the bonfire flames.

'Only one who ever leaves,' says Hark.

'Do you ever think of it, yourself?'

Hark shakes his head. 'Life's here, such as it is.'

'Thought I might ask him,' Firwit says. 'See if there's room for another in his boat, when spring comes.'

'And leave your sheep?' Hark leans to ruffle the sheepdog's fur where he lies at Firwit's feet.

'Eighteen years, it's been. Might have been yesterday, for all I've got to grips with it. If I'd married, it would be different. But I was good as married to Murnon.'

'Not reason enough to be off, I'd say.'

Firwit shrugs. 'Well, don't you make the same mistake. Why are you not married yet?'

They turn at a cry of delight and watch Marram and Iska bend to embrace their daughters, who come scampering from the gorse. The girls' hair glows coppery rich in the light, and Redwing frowns at them from where he munches on scallops nearby.

Firwit nudges Hark as Gertie Quirk dashes past, chasing her nephews with a monstrous growl.

'You might've asked that one,' Firwit says.

'It was Madden Lightfoot I hoped to ask.'

Firwit turns to peer at Hark in the gloom. 'Shame,' he says.

It was a bright night when Hark followed Madden up to the wood. His gut churned, from the vile mushroom tea Madden had made him drink as they left the house, and from the hunch that this was a mistake.

Madden grew wild as they crossed the hill, and the world grew wild with her. Tumbling leaves turned to waves, and the sky tilted over Hark's head, its starry eyes blinking at him. Madden ran ahead, stretching tall as the trees. She leapt long grass that deepened into bristling fur along the hill's ridge. Hark's legs slowed, heavy as mud, but somehow, soon, the wood rushed around them, deep, dazzling.

'We're here,' Madden called, her voice curling up and away.

They ducked beneath naked branches. Hark bent his head and clung to Madden, watching the ground leaves whiten in the moonlight haze.

Madden pulled him forward, further in, and two black trees moved to meet them. They were Guller, the bird man, and Murnon, the shepherd.

Guller held a sack, a hunch at his back. 'Glad to see you again, Madden. You drank?' he asked.

'Hark, too,' Madden said and went to take his arm. 'I hope he'll try tonight. I've told him what a gift it is you give.'

Guller grinned, his eyes like marbles. He stood only as high as Madden's shoulder, but Hark felt the urge to pull her away, to safety.

'One more to come tonight,' Guller's voice wheedled, 'but she'll find us.' He took Madden's hand and led them along the ash-pale path, Hark stumbling behind, the shepherd Murnon loping silent between them.

They reached a clearing, a great bowl of moonlight, stars dewy in the dark far above. Hark's stomach bubbled like broth. He tried to call Madden away from Guller, but she was opening the sack with him, pulling out bundles that unfolded in their hands. He knew what they were. She touched the feathers so easily, it made him shiver.

Murnon the shepherd held his shoulder. 'Steady,' he said, but the word echoed, far away. Murnon's face was old, the lines in it furrowed so deep by moon shadow, it seemed ancient stone. In the silver air, they all four sat, waiting.

'Don't you want to see? The kites,' Madden whispered, but Hark would not put out his hand to touch the mound of feathers in her lap. She turned it over, and spread the wings wide, so he could see the clean dried skin of the underside. He watched her take the white stone she wore on a thread around her neck and tuck it into the head of the kite skin. When she leaned and kissed Hark's cheek he felt the heat of her breath, and the brush of a wingtip on his bare arm.

'No sign of old Winfrid yet. So, you first, youngster?' Guller said, and Madden stood, a tall, thin shape beside the little man. Guller unspooled a length of cord. He tied one end around Madden's waist, and the other around a tree trunk at the clearing's edge, leaving the cord loose between them.

'What's that for?' Hark whispered to Murnon.

'A tether, lest she lose her way,' Murnon said. 'Brings her back.'

Hark could hear the thrill in Madden's breath, deep gusts that prickled alarm in his head, even as Guller began to whistle. Madden had told him how Guller made birdsong in his throat, but a chill struck him to hear the flute notes of a red kite flowing from a man.

The sound rose. It sent his mind high, clear of the trees, and he heard the whistle of other kites, threading the air. Madden spread the wings of her kite skin as wide as her arms would let her. Her knuckles were bone, gripping feathers as the kite skin rose, until she held it high above her head. Hark's stomach clenched.

Wing shadows flooded the floor of the clearing and the kites called on and on. Madden leaned backwards, the cord pulled taut from the tree, the wings in her hands seeming to beat as the kite strained upwards. The whole wood quivered. Hark saw the whites of Madden's eyes in the moonlight. Though she held the wings high in her strong hands, her legs trembled. He stood to go to her, to make Guller stop what was happening, but Guller shook his head. Soon, Hark saw Guller tug on the cord, pulling Madden forward. She dropped the kite skin and fell. Guller caught her shoulders and eased her down. She smiled as if in sleep.

Hark bent over her. 'Madden,' he tried, but Guller hushed him.

'She'll wake. She's been a long way, up there.'

Hark felt the chill of the wood's breath, the trees bending closer to stare at Madden. Her eyes opened. 'What was it like?' he asked, but she sat up and pressed her face hot into his neck.

Guller was beginning with Murnon now, tying the cord at his waist, the kite's whistle trailing from his lips.

'Bliss,' Madden whispered. 'You must try, Hark. It's just joy, flying up so high, the whole sky turning about you, no body to weigh you down. I wish I could stay up there forever, not just a few hours.'

'But it was moments,' Hark said.

'Please try. I want you to feel like that, better than anything.'

'Let's go home,' he said, but Madden was looking past him, at a figure taking slow steps into the clearing. It huddled against a tree and watched, while Guller spun out the kite's song and Murnon swayed, his own kite skin stretched high. Guller tugged the cord and caught Murnon as he fell, just as he had with Madden. Then he beckoned the bent figure over.

'It's been a long while. But you've made up your mind?' Guller said. The old woman nodded.

The wide grin faded from Guller's face. For the first time, he looked solemn. The two of them clasped their hands together in greeting for a long moment.

'Is that Winfrid Plait, from up by the river?' Hark asked Madden.

'Poor old thing's got nobody left. Hardly leaves her house, except to sit by that pool and mope.'

'Isn't she too old for all this?' Hark said. 'Come on, Madden, I've had enough.'

'Wait,' she said and turned to watch. Winfrid held the bird skin unsteady in the air, still nodding as Guller looped the cord around her waist. The eerie cries from the sky pierced Hark's head, and Guller's whistling grew higher, sweeter than before. The shaking in Winfrid's arms calmed, and the wings she held stretched wider. It went on, all of them held in the web of sound that filled the clearing. Still Guller did not tug on the cord, to pull Winfrid back to ground. Hark felt Madden's hand gripping his own. He heard her gasp when Guller took a knife from his pocket and cut clean through the tether.

Hark's head spun, and his gut roiled, as he and Madden stumbled home across the hill. Before they reached the village, he retched and emptied the burning tea from his stomach.

After Guller had cut the tether, he had laid Winfrid down, still but warm, breathing, in a bed of dead leaves. He had placed the kite skin under her head. Winfrid was already gone, he had said, and it would not take long, here in the wood, for her body to turn cold. The burial would be done later.

'Up there, forever?' Madden had asked, and Guller nodded. 'I didn't know you could do that,' she'd said, and the joy in her face had opened a well in Hark that filled with cold, black water.

'Why not?' Madden asked the next day. She stood below Hark with the bucket while he climbed the ladder and painted whitewash on to the wall of the house. The low autumn sun warmed his back, but Madden's mood, and her words, stirred the dark water that still lay cold inside him.

'Don't be a dunce,' he said.

'But why not? If you could choose endless joy, bliss that never, ever wore out, wouldn't you?' Madden said, waving the bucket in her hand and sloshing whitewash into the weeds.

'I'm happy enough.'

'You wouldn't be if you'd tried it. You'd know then, what real happiness was like.'

'I do know.' Hark leaned down to dip the brush.

'What then. When do you feel it?'

'When I sit with you by the fire. When I eat a good bit of roast meat and talk with my brothers of an evening. Or just this, sun in a blue sky and making a good job of it.' He turned to dip the brush again, and wiped sweat from his forehead. 'Don't sneer, Madden.'

'Those are such small things. And besides, you might lose them.'

'I might lose you?'

'That's the trouble with sleepwalkers. Never know where they'll end up.' She shook her head. 'And you'd be all right without me. You always grumble that I'm a misery, anyway.'

'I'd like it if you were happy. If you could be. Wouldn't you be happier if you went back to work at the High Farm? You loved those horses.'

Madden grimaced. 'I tell you how I'd be happy. If I could go up, flying with the kites, and never had to come back.'

'And what about me?'

'Come and try it. Tonight.'

'You're going back again, already?' Hark stared at her. She put the bucket down. 'Of course,' she said. 'If you'd any sense at all, you'd come too.'

'I'm the only one with any sense,' he called after her as she went into the house and slammed the door shut.

Hark lay awake in the pitch of their room. There was a shadow side to Madden that had always frightened him. It had been there even when they were young and Madden had taught him to ride up at the High Farm. She was so sure of herself with the horses, but sometimes she was more fierce than strong. Hark knew she had night terrors, and that after her father died, she sometimes went to the cave at the far shore end at night. She said that if she didn't, she'd dream her father's death, his fall from those rocks, and that would be far worse than sitting and thinking of it purposely.

Now they were grown, and Hark had got himself this house. He'd planned to ask Madden if she would marry him, though he hadn't much hope she'd say yes. He'd seen the way Robin Prowd looked at her, up at the farm, with a kind of sad wanting in his eyes. Hark had been secretly pleased when whatever bond they'd had was broken, and Madden arrived at his house with a sack of her things, cursing Robin, asking if she might stay. She couldn't go home, she'd said through clenched teeth. Hark had felt her shoulders soften as he put his arms around her.

So now here she was, sharing his house. She trusted him, and he loved her. If he was calm where she was moody, if he planned where she tried not to think of what fate might bring, then he believed he could do her good. He had never forsaken her, through years of wildness and slumps of despair. Even when his brother, Dally, had warned him, said she'd make misery for him and he should court a merrier girl, he'd stuck with her. He wanted the chance to make her happy again.

It was dawn when he was woken by Madden, crawling into the bed beside him. She was cold, shivery, and he rubbed warmth into her back.

'It was so beautiful, Hark,' she whispered.

He held on to her, keeping as still as he could, until she slept.

He'd finished with the whitewashing and was stacking stones to repair the half-tumbled garden wall by the time Madden rose. It was another fine day, and Hark was pleased with his work. The house that had been a wreck when he took it on would be ready for their first winter together, cosy as doves.

'Why are you bothering with that?' Madden asked, when she found him heaving a large stone into a gap. She looked pale, and weary.

'Same reason I bother with anything. For you, to make our life good.' He pushed the stone, to wedge it into place, and it rolled and fell on the far side of the wall.

Madden huffed. 'You shouldn't.'

He followed her into the house where she sank into a chair and leaned her head on her arm. 'You'll get like an owl, up all night and asleep all day,' he called, while he washed his hands. He heard her laugh.

'It's a kite I want to be like,' she said, when he came and sat beside her.

Hark breathed deep. 'Please, Madden, will you not go again? It's a worry to me.'

'And what about me?'

'Let me make you happy, not Guller and his foul tea and dead birds.' He thought of Winfrid and took another deep breath. 'I do love you, Madden.'

She sank lower in the chair. 'If you loved me, you'd let me do it. You'd let me choose the same as Winfrid, wouldn't you? You're just being selfish.'

Hark grabbed her hands, though she tried to pull away. 'You want to be like that old woman, a corpse in a heap of leaves? You don't know that her soul is flying forever, that she has this bliss you keep talking about. It's trickery. Guller is playing with you.'

'Guller helped her,' Madden said, fierce. 'And it's not a trick. It feels real.'

'As real as this? Your hands in my hands, here, in our house?'

'Yes. Winfrid is lucky.' She spat the words, and Hark wanted to twist her hands, to force her to see what was real, what was not, but he couldn't hurt her.

'Don't deny me it,' she said. Her face began to crumple. When she wept, Hark held her shoulders and soothed her, and when that night she tied on her boots and set out for the wood, he did not stop her.

Every night for a whole week, Madden went to the wood, and came home at dawn to sleep until noon. Every day, Hark hunted for things to cheer her. He went to see Dally and begged the best bits of meat from the Oxley herd to tempt her to eat. He chopped logs and kept the fire up, because Madden liked to be warm. He tried to talk to her, and make her say that there were good things in life, so he could tell her he would always bring them. He would do whatever she wanted.

But Madden would not go along with it. Always, she said there was only one way to be happy, that only a fool would not take it. She did not eat the food he gave her. She sat in the chair, or lay in the bed, and waited for dusk. One night, ragged with despair, Hark tried to hold her back when she got ready to leave. He stood before the door, gripped her arms to her sides, and shook her. But she only twisted from his grasp and loped from the house barefoot.

Hark leaned in the doorway, too ashamed to follow her, the night air cooling his cheeks. He looked at the stars for the first time since he had been in the wood with her, and they had seemed to watch. Madden was right, they were beautiful, but they were cold, and silent.

He tried to eat but couldn't. He dug inside the trunk for more blankets, to warm Madden up when she came home, and found the bottle of Guller's toadstool tea. The smell of it made his stomach turn, and he remembered how strange the world had seemed when he'd drunk from it, how the sounds dimmed or echoed, and the wood lost its familiar pattern in ripples. If he had wanted to believe in magic, he could have, then. But magic was dishonesty, and Guller was a liar, even if Madden enjoyed the lie. It could not be real.

He took the bottle outside, ready to empty it on to the ground, but the sound of a kite's whistle reached him and turned his blood icy. He threw the bottle into the grass and ran.

It was easy to find the clearing, though the light from the moon was not pearly as it had been before. There was a rustle in the undergrowth nearby, and he called, 'Madden,' only for the wood to fall silent. Then he saw her, lying beneath the low branches of an elder bush. She was smiling, but when he shook her, she would not wake. There was a kite skin tucked beneath her head.

Madden had still not woken by the time Hark reached the house, his arms roaring from carrying her, his heart thudding as he ran and scrambled down the hill. When he had laid her in the chair, he wet her lips with whisky, then poured from the cup into each of their mouths. Her eyelids did not even flicker. He nested her in blankets, whispered her name, then yelled it. The beat of blood where he touched her neck was steady, her breath quiet but sure.

'What have you done?' he asked her, and then turned the question on himself, over and over, all through the night.

When dawn came, he hoped the light might stir Madden, but still she slept. He called her, and shook her, in vain. It was to Guller's house he hurried first.

'Tell me how to bring her back,' he shouted, as he pushed the door and fell into the room. It stank of decay, and feathers shifted across the floor in the draught. A magpie shrieked above his head. Guller stood at his table, cleaning a bird's skull. He looked at Hark as he spat again on a cloth and dabbed at the bone.

'You can't do that,' he said, his voice singsong like a child's.

'Then you do it,' said Hark.

Guller shook his head and smiled. 'Not me, neither. She's gone.'

'She's not dead. She's only asleep.' Hark stepped closer to the table, where the bones and innards of a large bird were spread in stained heaps.

'She was sure, you know. You should be glad for her,' Guller said, his round marble eyes holding Hark's gaze. 'Bliss.'

Hark reached out and dashed the bird skull from Guller's hand. It skittered across the floor in pieces.

'Careful,' Guller said.

'If she doesn't wake, if she dies, you've killed her. Poisoned her, with that drink of toadstools, and with lies dressed up as magic.'

'But she lives.' Guller moved away from the table to peer up at the sky through the rimed window. 'It's only that she's no need for a body now. When it grows cold, it will make no difference to her. Bliss,' he repeated. 'Wouldn't you wish her that?'

'I'll tell everyone what you've done. Her mother, all the village,' Hark said.

Guller opened his arms, as if in belated welcome. 'Spread the word,' he said. 'I'm the only one who can give them stars, all that joy, on high. Elders, youngsters, all kinds come.'

'Not to die.'

'No, but sometimes to stay, up there. Old Winfrid Plait, she chose it. And you know Ervet? Her father, Berry.' Guller grinned, his eyes rolling before they fixed on Hark, sidelong. 'I can make you see why Madden wanted it. The price is only small,' and he jingled the coins in his pocket.

'A low price?' Hark yelled. He kicked at the table and the bird bones shuddered. 'She's given up her life.'

'No, no,' Guller said, and he laughed. 'Try it. You'll see.'

But Hark was already out of the door, spitting the stench of the house from his mouth.

If it's a lie, she will wake, he told himself, as he hurried back home, wincing at the sun that dazzled his tired eyes. If I keep her warm, feed her, give her drink, she'll come round. But the blackberries he mashed for Madden only lay on her tongue, and the milk he poured trickled from her lips.

He searched the kite skin, which he'd carried home with Madden, for clues to undo the spell. When he nudged Madden's white stone from inside the kite's head, a slip of paper fell out with it. On it was scratched a drawing of a tree with two thick branches. It was the one they used to climb when they were still children, and Madden would dare Hark to leap from its crook.

Holding the kite skin in his hands, he felt the power in the wings, the urge to fly, even though it was empty. He could not go back to Guller. He could not tell his brothers. Then he remembered Murnon the shepherd.

Hark found Murnon up at the edge of the sheep field, sitting in a nook in the stone wall. Cloud hung low now, above the hill, and no birdsong disturbed the air. The shepherd nodded as Hark left the path to join him.

'Not as foolish as they seem, those goings-on with Guller,' he said, before Hark even asked his question. He shifted and made room for him to sit on the wall.

'Why do you do it?' asked Hark.

Murnon pointed behind with his thumb at the huddle of sheep in the field. 'I'm glad enough to do my work, but I know my flock so well, there's nothing to keep my mind from turning black, often. The kites, they're my relief. Show me there's more, when I see only gloom in life.'

'More?'

'Something greater. Real joy, and joy that harms nobody to take. Guller means no ill, and folk need some comfort.'

Hark shook his head. 'But it's not real. It's just toad-stool dreaming.'

'A dream's as real as life, for the dreamer. What's the difference?'

Hark thought about the house, all the mending and patching he'd done. That was real, solid. It was all for Madden, for their life together. 'If you really think that, why haven't you done what Winfrid did?'

'And your Madden.'

Hark's throat tightened.

'My brother, Firwit,' said Murnon. 'He'd be as useless as half a horse on his own. I do the flock, see, and when it comes to it, the slaughter, the meat. Firwit handles the skins. Same in the house. Left to it, he'd not know what to do. I can bear it, long as I can get to the woods at night.'

'I wanted to share, too. With Madden,' Hark said.

Murnon nodded. 'Well. She wanted her freedom.'

Hark bent forward, his face pressed into his hands, his palms hot and wet. He felt Murnon grip his shoulder, as he had in the wood.

'You can scorn an old man's opinion if you want, but I'd go up, once, with the kites. You might feel better. You might even forgive her.'

All the rest of that long day and night, Hark sat with Madden, or paced the house, finding tasks that needed doing, then seeing the pointlessness of doing them. He didn't want to leave her, but neither did he want to be there when the last life went from her body. The only comfort he could find, in the end, was that she was not suffering with him. It was hard to keep hold of this thought. It sank over and over into the deep black well.

Finally, worn out with fidgeting, he spoke to Murnon and agreed to come to the wood the next night. He found the bottle of brown tea lying in the grass and drank from it, standing before Madden, to show her he was doing what she had wanted. Then he waited for the world to begin to ripple, tucked the kite skin under his arm and wandered over the darkening hill, under the blinking eyes of the stars.

By the time he greeted Murnon and Guller, the wood had become a whispering maze, and he followed them with halting steps between black trunks that loomed, the reaching fingers of bramble tripping his feet. The stars that crowded above the clearing were sparking, now that the moon had waned to a sliver. Hark wanted to vomit, but held his stomach, willing the tea to help work Guller's spell. He willed it to conjure Madden, bold and joyous, before it was all over with.

He could not make out Guller's features as he tied the cord at his waist. He seemed to grin and frown, go from kind to scornful. Hark heard Guller's words as if from within his own head.

'You've put something of yours inside the skin?'

'My handkerchief.'

'Use that. Put yourself inside the kite. Let it take you up. I'll keep you tethered, here, till it's time to return.'

Hark did not tell Guller that his handkerchief was wrapped around Madden's white stone.

He closed his eyes and listened for the whistling. The thin, quivering sound washed away all thought. There were just the feather tips in his fingers, the wing shadows wheeling, somewhere, everywhere, the call to rise. The kite skin spread wider, the secret beat of its wings thrummed through his arms, and the clearing was gone, closed into the wood below him.

It was true. He hadn't words for anything then, but afterwards he had to call it bliss. A sweetness familiar and new, a delight with no shape. How long he flew, drinking in the pleasure of starlight, he didn't know. In the last moment, as he felt himself falling, the tether pulling him down to earth, he heard Madden's voice, close in his ear and then fading far above. *Stay*, she said.

Hark sat up, was sick into the dead leaves, and lay back down. The trees bent over him, but more kindly now. Murnon and Guller murmured somewhere nearby. He lay, waiting for Madden, for her voice, some trace, but there was nothing after all.

After he had taken Madden's note to the Lightfoot house, Hark carried her body back across the hill to the woods. Clouds were wadded thick above him, and the night whispers of the trees had faded to a familiar hush. He chose a place where no hunters would walk, where the beech leaves lay deep, and their red-brown glow suggested warmth to him. He laid Madden down.

'I know now,' he said, as he tucked more leaves around her. 'I still think you're wrong, but why would you listen to me?' He sat beside her, with her white stone in his hand. He waited a long time there in the greying dusk, letting go his last hope, before he set off home again.

He could see the whitewashed house as he crossed the hill, half-made and empty, gleaming as the world around it faded. He dreaded the dark night in his bed, and worse, the plain light of morning. As he came closer, he saw a shadow lying across the stone step at his door. He stared down at the kite skin, wings folded beneath it, the head tucked down into the empty breast. He picked it up and carried it inside.

'Girls are all down.' Firwit points to where Orta and the others are brandishing their bows, beginning their wagers on whose kiss each will get. 'Boys'll be up in the tunnels now. Never did see the Gorse Mother when I was young.'

But Hark is not listening. The sky above their heads is showing the first stars. He gazes up and wonders how many turns they've made through the dark while he has watched them and thought of Madden. How many times he has set out for the woods with the kite skin, only to turn back home.

He takes up a torch, and waits with the other men and women of Neverness. The door of the day is nearly shut, but this is the hinge of the year itself. The boys and girls have been paired up, a kiss for each arrow shot deep in the gorse. They lead each other off into the night, or sit shyly by the bonfire under Firwit's watchful eye.

The line of flame begins its march, with Hark taking last place. The hill is black. The only light flows orange from the torches now. As the villagers spread out around the gorse, there is a whisper along the row on the seaward side. *Gorse Mother. Gold Mother.* Gill Skerry does not join in the chant.

The torches lean in closer, their flames swooping in the wind. The first licks take. Soon the headland of Neverness is crackling, spitting fire into the sky, as cheers go up through the scented smoke.

ACKNOWLEDGEMENTS

To each and every one below, a great big thank you for the role you played in making this book spring into existence. If I haven't repaid you yet, I hope I will get the chance:

Alison MacLeod, my fantastic PhD supervisor, teacher and mentor.

All the wonderful writers who have taught me at Arvon and Ty Newydd courses, especially Jane Feaver, Helen Oyeyemi, Jon McGregor, Tania Hershman, Sara Maitland and David Constantine; and Kevin Crossley-Holland, who told me I could do it.

Alexa von Hirschberg, my clear-eyed, passionate editor, and all the people at Bloomsbury who have made this book beautiful, including Alexandra Pringle, Imogen Denny, Marigold Atkey, Callum Kenny, Francesca Sturiale, David Mann and Sarah-Jane Forder.

My aunt Isobel Simonds, whose wonderful imagination and skill created the illustrations that grace these pages.

Lucy Luck, my agent-with-aplomb.

Cathy Galvin and everyone at the Word Factory.

All my critique-group comrades past and present at the North London Writers' Group, my own Short Story Critique Group, and at the Brick Lane bookshop.

All the other writers who have read and commented and cheered me on; I can't name you all here, but especially Lily Dunn.

Adam Marek, for reading and supporting tirelessly, thank you.

My whole creative and inspiring family, believers in making; who are kind about my make-believe.

My mother, who believes in fairies: this book is for you because I can't thank you enough.

All the editors who commissioned, or selected for publication, versions of some of the tales that make up this book: Ra Page of Comma Press for commissioning 'Tether' for *Thought X: Fiction and Hypotheticals* and 'Thunder Cracks' for *Spindles*; Jan Fortune of Cinnamon Press for selecting 'Sticks are for Fire' for *Journey Planner and Other Stories and Poems* and 'Mawkin' (which formed the basis for 'Fishskin, Hareskin') for *Patria*; Deborah McMenamy of Labello Press for selecting 'The Neverness Ox-men' for *Gem Street*; the editors at *Glint* journal for publishing 'Earth is Not for Eating'; everyone at the Mechanics' Institute Review for including 'Kite' in issue 12; Hilary Mantel and David Rogers for selecting 'Water Bull Bride' for *What Lies Beneath*; the Costa Short Story Prize (and all those who voted) for making 'Fishskin, Hareskin' a winner, and commissioning the beautiful audio version on the Costa website.

Lastly, the entire Isle of Man, a place of gorse-scented inspiration and fantastic folk tales.

Zoe Gilbert is the winner of the Costa Short Story
Award 2014. Her work has appeared in anthologies
from Comma, Cinnamon, Labello and Pankhearst
presses, and has been published in journals including
*The Stinging Fly, Mechanics' Institute Review, Bohemyth,
Lighthouse* and the *British Fantasy Society Journal.* She
has taken part in writing projects in China and South
Korea for the British Council and was commissioned
by Microsoft to create a short story book in collabo-
ration with graphic artist Isabel Greenberg. She is
completing a PhD in Fiction and Creative Writing
at the University of Chichester, focusing on folk tales
in contemporary fiction. She co-hosts the Short Story
Club at the Word Factory and is the co-founder of
London Lit Lab, providing creative writing courses for
Londoners. She lives on a hill in South London.

A NOTE ON THE TYPE

The text of this book is set in Adobe Caslon, named after the English punch-cutter and type-founder William Caslon I (1692–1766). Caslon's rather old-fashioned types were modelled on seventeenth-century Dutch designs, but found wide acceptance throughout the English-speaking world for much of the eighteenth century until replaced by newer types towards the end of the century. Used in 1776 to print the Declaration of Independence, they were revived in the nineteenth century and have been popular ever since, particularly amongst fine printers. There are several digital versions, of which Carol Twombly's Adobe Caslon is one.